ALSO BY KRISTEN TRACY

Crimes of the Sarahs
Hung Up

Lost It

KRISTEN TRACY

Simon Pulse

New York   London   Toronto   Sydney   New Delhi

This book is a work of fiction. Any references to historical events,
real people, or real places are used fictitiously. Other names, characters,
places, and events are products of the author's imagination, and
any resemblance to actual events or places or persons,
living or dead, is entirely coincidental.

MM SIMON PULSE
An imprint of Simon & Schuster Children's Publishing Division
1230 Avenue of the Americas, New York, NY 10020
First Simon Pulse paperback edition January 2007
This Simon Pulse paperback edition March 2014
Copyright © 2007 by Kristen Tracy
For information about special discounts for bulk purchases,
please contact Simon & Schuster Special Sales at 1-866-506-1949
or business@simonandschuster.com.
The Simon & Schuster Speakers Bureau can bring authors
to your live event. For more information or to book an event contact
the Simon & Schuster Speakers Bureau at 1-866-248-3049 or
visit our website at www.simonspeakers.com.
Designed by Mike Rosamilia
The text of this book was set in Scala OT.
Manufactured in the United States of America
10 9 8 7 6 5 4 3 2 1
Library of Congress Control Number 2006928453
ISBN 978-1-4424-8102-2 (pbk)
ISBN 978-1-4391-0692-1 (eBook)

For my grandmothers,
Helen Cleopatra Newman and Lois Sophia Ritchie Tracy,
both of whom were very generous and religious women.
No doubt they each would have been surprised by parts
of this story, but they would have loved me anyway.

ACKNOWLEDGMENTS

I would like to thank Sara Crowe, who believed in this book and worked hard to find it the perfect home. I'm also incredibly grateful to Michelle Nagler, whose care and comments helped turn this manuscript into a much better version of itself. Ultimately, Tess's story is the product of years of encouragement and generous guidance from my many mentors and friends. My sincere thanks go out to Gail Wronsky, Brian Evenson, Darrell Spencer, Kathryn Davis, Eric Zencey, Sydney Lea, Stephen Dunn, Ellen Lesser, Rick Zand, Michelle Willis, Linda Young, Ulla Frederiksen, Al Young, and Stuart Dybek. I am very fortunate to have come across such a thoughtful and talented bunch of folks. I would also like to thank the Arts Council of Greater Kalamazoo and the Irving S. Gilmore Emerging Artist Grant for their generous support. Last, but definitely not least, I must thank my sister, mother, and father for their friendship and constant support. They're the best.

Chapter 1

I didn't start out my junior year of high school planning to lose my virginity to Benjamin Easter—a senior—at his parents' cabin in Island Park underneath a sloppily patched, unseaworthy, upside-down canoe. Up to that point in my life, I'd been somewhat of a prude who'd avoided the outdoors, especially the wilderness, for the sole purpose that I didn't want to be eaten alive.

I'm from Idaho. The true West. And if there's a beast indigenous to North America that can kill you, it probably lives here. My whole life, well-meaning people have tried to alleviate my fear of unpredictable, toothy carnivores.

But I was never fooled by the pamphlets handed to me by tan-capped park rangers during the seven-day camping trip that my parents forced upon me every summer. The tourist literature wanted you to believe that you were safe as long as you hung your food in a tree and didn't try to snap pictures of the buffalo within goring distance. Seriously, when in the presence of a buffalo, isn't *any* distance within goring distance?

And they expect intelligent people to believe that a bear can't smell menstrual blood? A bear's nose is more sensitive than a dog's. Every Westerner knows that. In my opinion, if you're having your period and you're stupid enough to pitch a tent in Yellowstone Park, you're either crazy or suicidal. Maybe both.

It's clear why losing my virginity outdoors, in the wilderness, with Benjamin Easter should be taken as an enormous shock. I could have been eaten by a mountain lion, mauled by a grizzly bear, or (thanks to some people my father refers to as "troublemaking tree huggers") torn to pieces by a pack of recently relocated gray wolves.

Of course, I wasn't. To be completely honest, I may be overstating the actual risk that was involved. It happened in December. The bears were all hibernating. And the event didn't end up taking that long. Plus, like I already said, we were hidden underneath a canoe.

But the fact that I lost it in a waterproof sleeping bag on top of a patch of frozen dirt with Benjamin Easter is something that I'm still coming to terms with.

I can't believe it. Even though I've had several days to process the event. I let a boy see me completely naked, and by this I mean braless and without my underpants. I let a boy I'd known for less than four months bear witness to the fact that my right breast was slightly smaller than my left one. And would I do it again?

We did do it again. After the canoe, in the days that followed, we did it two more times. I remember them well. Honestly, I remember them *very* well. Each moment is etched into my mind like a petroglyph. After the third and final time, I watched as he rolled his body away from mine. With my ring finger, I tussled his curly brown hair. Then, I fell asleep. When I woke up, Ben was dressed again, kissing me good-bye. I find myself returning to this moment often. Like it's frozen in time. Sadly, you can't actually freeze time.

Last night, Ben told me, "You're acting outrageous." He said this while inserting a wooden spoon into the elbow-end of my plaster cast. He was trying to rescue the hamster. The hamster had been my idea. I'd just bought it for him. I wanted him to take it to college and always think of me, his broken-armed first love. But the rodent had weaseled its way into my cast. I hadn't realized that hamsters were equipt with burrowing instincts. I also had no idea how to make a boy stay in love with me. Hence, the pet hamster.

It's been hours since I've talked to Ben. Since the hamster episode. And the argument that followed the hamster episode. That night Ben told me to stop calling him. He was serious. I told him to have a happy New Year. And he hung up on me. The boy I'd lost it with in a sleeping bag in the frozen dirt had left me with nothing but a dial tone.

I swear, the day I woke up and started my junior year of high school, Benjamin Easter wasn't even on my radar. I didn't know a thing about leukemia. And because I was raised by deeply conservative people, who wouldn't let me wear mascara or attend sex education classes at Rocky Mountain High School, I wasn't even aware that I had a hymen or that having sex would break it.

Actually, in the spirit of full disclosure and total honesty, I should mention that my parents only became born-again rather recently, at about the time I hit puberty, following a serious grease fire in the kitchen. Before that, they only ventured to church on major holidays. Hence, my life became much more restricted and we gave up eating deep-fried foods.

The day I started my junior year, I woke up worrying about the size of my feet. Once dressed, looking at myself in my full-length bedroom mirror, they struck me as incredibly long and boatlike. I squished them into a pair of shoes I'd worn in eighth grade, brown suede loafers. They pinched, but gave my feet the illusion of looking regular-size instead of Cadillac-size. Then I noticed a newly risen zit. Of course, under the cover of darkness, it had cowardly erupted in the center of my forehead. I held back my brown bangs and popped it. Then I dabbed the surrounding area with a glob of beige-colored Zit-Be-Gone cream.

I started the first day of my junior year of high school zitless and basically happy. I was sixteen and feeling good. I didn't have any major issues. Okay, that's not entirely true. For weeks I'd been growing increasingly concerned about Zena Crow, my overly dramatic best friend. She'd been going through a rocky stretch and had been talking incessantly about building a bomb. Not a big bomb. Just one that was big enough to blow up a poodle.

Chapter 2

The day started out the same way as the first day of my freshman and sophomore years. I stood at my front door, pressed into that small space between the screen and the door itself. This was how I waited for Zena. Initially, I had waited to be picked up in my driveway. But standing there, alone, in the dull morning light, made me feel way too vulnerable. I always thought of the wildlife out there that I couldn't see: foxes slipping through hay fields, weasels hunting for farm cats or chickens, a rogue coyote scouting to take down any available prey. Why I had chosen to live my life in total fear of the wilderness was a mystery to even myself.

I pressed my nose to the screen's mesh, closed my eyes, and listened for the sound of Zena's squeaky brakes. Fortunately, the summer before my freshman year, the local newspaper had printed an article that explored the seedy underbelly of school bus violence, highlighting a recent incident in New Jersey where a Popsicle stick had been whittled to a point and used as a shiv. After that, my parents practically insisted that I ride with Zena. Hence, I was on my third year of being ferried to school via Zena and her Mercury.

In Idaho, the law states that you can get your driver's license at fifteen. Upon learning this, my California-born parents stated that I could get my driver's license when I was able to afford my own car insurance. Collision and comprehensive.

Ironically, when I turned fourteen, they did let me take driver's ed. I think it was because the instructor had a reputation for showing videos that featured horrific car accidents. So the summer before my freshman year, I watched shot after shot of accordioned metal. Then came the testimonials. In one, a boy—still in traction—swore that he never should have been eating a cinnamon roll while attempting to make a three-point turn. For forty-five minutes the injured and maimed pleaded with us to turn down our radios and buckle up.

Then, the video closed with a montage of headstones, carefully zooming in on the birth and death dates, letting us know that beneath each stone marker lay a fallen fellow teen. Zena thought the video crossed a line. That it could steer the truly skittish among us right into becoming Amish. She made a good point. Still, at the end of that summer, for Tess Whistle, there was no license. There was no car.

Zena's parents, on the other hand, had given her a green Mercury Cougar the second she turned fifteen. She took me everywhere, never charging gas money. And I assumed that she would pick me up and cart me around until the day I graduated. Go ahead and call me naive.

As I stood in between my screen and front door, in my tight loafers, I don't think I had a single interesting thought running through my head. High school, for me, was a boring routine that I was forced to endure in order to get into the college of my choice: UCLA, a university located away from my parents and close to the ocean. Zena felt similarly. But she was interested in the opposite coast. She hoped to attend Barnard College in New York City, which she insisted was the better school.

Zena picked me up on time and things were pretty much normal. Her radio only plucked AM waves from the air, so we listened to bubblegum rock from the fifties all the way to school. Actually, Zena turned down the radio several times to discuss newly realized obstacles in making her bomb.

"One of my catalogs warns that, considering my ingredients, it's tough to avoid creating shrapnel. But I'm not interested in taking down any bystanders. I'm only after the poodle."

I nodded. Frankly, I didn't know what else to do. Of course, I didn't approve of her blowing up an animal. I guess I figured that the actual construction of the bomb was still in its early stages. I mean, the poodle could die of natural causes before Zena ever got the thing built. But it was a good sign that she was concerned about innocent people in the general vicinity of the blast zone. It was the first time she'd mentioned them. I wanted to say something more to Zena in defense of the poodle, but when I turned to confront her, her face looked so sad that I didn't. I turned and looked back out the windshield.

Zena was an excellent driver. She gripped the steering wheel at ten and two o'clock and never took her eyes off of the road. Her eyes were one of her most attractive features—forest green with flecks of gold in them.

As Zena drove down the Yellowstone Highway to school, it was easy not to take her too seriously. Until last month, until the poodle had become her target, she'd been hung up on building a nuclear bomb. Everybody knows how hard it is for a teenager to purchase radioactive material. Then, overnight, she readjusted her aim and decided to blow up a small, furry dog instead. It came across as a joke. Even though Zena never laughed when talking about it.

"I want to blow it up soon, Tess," Zena said, aiming the Mercury into an empty parking stall.

"I want advance warning," I said, unbuckling my safety belt.

Zena turned her thin body to face me.

"Tess, I promise to give you advance warning." She took my hand and gave it a strong squeeze.

I can't say that this promise made me feel completely better, but it did take off some of the pressure. There wasn't going to be any detonating without a warning. I guess I figured that deep down I could talk her out of it, that at the last moment I'd somehow be able to stop her.

We walked together into the windowless, brick building, our backpacks slipping off our shoulders. (Anybody who'd erect a brick building that blocked out all natural sunlight should have his or her head examined.)

Once inside, we went to a large table in the center of the commons to get our locker assignments. The commons was stuffed with sophomores, juniors, and seniors. Some—mostly sophomores—looked confused, while others looked tired. A large clump of seniors looked bored. Zena said they were stoned. I thought she was kidding. Again, because I came from a household run by two certifiable prudes, I'd never been to a single high school party or seen a human being who was high before. I'd never seen a drunk person either. Except on network television. But those people weren't really drunk, they were just acting.

Zena was assigned a bottom locker. I was fortunate enough to be given a top one.

"I'm taller than you," Zena complained, setting her backpack down and rummaging around for a pen. "And I wear short skirts. I can't be bending over all the time."

I shrugged. We may have been best friends, but I wasn't about to surrender my conveniently positioned upper metal storage cage for her inconveniently situated lower one. Zena huffed at me and walked back to her locker, which wasn't anywhere near mine. Alphabetically speaking, Crow and Whistle were too far apart. This is where fate stepped in. Easter should have been closer to Crow. Easter shouldn't have been anywhere near Whistle. But because Ben Easter registered late, he ended up with the locker below mine, the one intended for Dudley Wiseman, who'd recently been hospitalized. His parents kept the nature of his condition vague. I suspected it was related to his psoriasis. Nobody heard a thing about him all semester.

I went to my top locker and noticed Ben Easter crouching down to open his bottom locker. His butt was sticking way out. I noticed his butt right away. I had never really noticed a guy's rear end before. I'm not some freak hung up on posteriors. I'm not even sure if I was attracted to him at this point or not. All I knew was that I thought his backside was nice-looking.

Okay, I need to be honest. I knew I liked him. The way his jeans hugged his cheeks drew me to him and made me feel warm. And unusually light. That's when I realized I'd dumped all eight of my spiral notebooks, ten pens, four very sharp pencils, a dinky plastic pencil sharpener, and a chilled can of apple juice on his head.

You know you're dealing with a classy guy when, after you've clobbered him, knocking him down to the freshly polished floor, he apologizes for being in the way and then picks up your things.

"I'm so sorry," I said. "It was an accident. A total accident."

"Apple juice?" he asked, handing me back my can.

For some reason the apple juice made me feel like a horrendous nerd. Apple juice was for babies. Why couldn't I have dropped a Diet Coke on him? Why didn't I drink Diet Coke? Well, I was sure going to start, aspartame or not.

In my mind, the only thing that would have been worse than clunking him on the head with a can of apple juice was clunking him on the head with an enormous baby bottle filled with breast milk. I returned the can to my backpack. I felt ashamed. And juvenile. So I told an unnecessary lie.

"I'm a diabetic," I said. "I was feeling woozy. That's why I dropped my things."

I don't know where this lie came from. I'd never even met anyone with diabetes before. But it worked. Ben Easter looked very concerned. He gathered the rest of my things and offered to open my locker for me.

"I don't give out my combo," I said.

Ben smiled. I remember thinking his lips looked soft. Several perfectly formed brown curls fell like fringe onto his forehead, landing just above his light blue eyes.

"I didn't mean to suggest that you did," he answered.

I thought his reply was very adult. He seemed much more mature than the rest of the male high school baboons. That's when he reached out his hand and wanted to shake my hand and introduce himself so we could greet each other like two civilized human beings and learn each other's names so we could start dating, exclusively, of course, and be together forever, and have highly attractive and intelligent babies that we'd name after presidents. But not any of the ones who were assassinated. Because that would be too weird.

"My name's Ben Easter. I'm from Michigan. I have a friend back home who has diabetes. If you ever need anything, let me know."

I nodded. He waited. I nodded again. Then he nodded back. I kept nodding. He slammed his locker and walked off.

Yes, it was going to be very difficult for us to start dating each other exclusively considering I hadn't even told Ben Easter my name. But this is where fate stepped in again. He learned it five minutes later in junior AP English. He sat in front of me. Zena sat behind me. Mrs. Hovel blew her nose and scribbled on the board in pale yellow chalk. I watched the back of Ben Easter's curly brown-haired head, while Mrs. Hovel announced that she was going to reintroduce us to gerunds. Then the bell rang and my junior year began.

Chapter 3

Even though zena claimed on numerous occasions to be clairvoyant, I was certain she was just putting me on. Then, two weeks into our junior year, while we were at my house popping red seedless grapes into our mouths, she said something that upon reflection convinced me that she does possess a certain degree of psychic power.

"Tess Whistle, you are so hot for Ben. How long do you think until you hook up with him and officially get laid?"

When Zena said "get laid," I nearly died. Seriously. A grape lodged in my windpipe, and Zena had to perform the Heimlich maneuver. She grabbed me from behind and pulled her fist into my stomach. On the third thrust, I spat out the grape, and it shot across the room at a high rate of speed, knocking my mother's favorite pickle dish off the shelf.

I coughed and stared at the pieces. There were a lot of them.

"Relax. You can reassemble it using airplane glue," Zena said.

I got a glass of water and tried to clear my throat. I even did some gargling. I must have released a sound that sounded like a dissenting opinion.

"You're right," Zena said. "That thing is beyond airplane glue."

I swallowed hard and caught my breath. Then I launched into my defense, which had nothing to do with the effectiveness of adhesives.

"I don't believe in getting laid. And you know that I want to wait until after I'm married, or at least engaged, until I'm officially in love, until after I have a ring." I coughed a little, which made my argument seem less persuasive. Then I stomped back into the kitchen, red-faced, and grabbed the trash can.

I used to be 100 percent certain that I'd wait until I was married before I had sex, but recently Zena had convinced me that an official engagement was nearly the same thing.

"That is so lame," Zena said. She fell back onto the couch and resumed eating the grapes. "You should've been alive during the fifties. Back then, pretending to be pure was fashionable. Now, people just find it annoying."

"I'm not trying to impress anyone. Why not wait until you know you're with somebody you love?" I said, lifting the broken pickle dish piece by piece into the trash can.

"A ring doesn't mean love," she said. "Unless your finger swells, it slips right off. Besides, love doesn't last. People fall in and out of it all the time. You've heard the sayings. Love hurts. Love dies. Love bites."

"A ring means something. And sometimes love does last," I said.

"Sometimes frozen airplane waste falls through the sky and rips through a roof and lands in a living room in Indiana and a housewife thinks she's found a meteorite. But all she's really got is a wad of frozen crap."

"What does that have to do with love?"

"Life is crazy. If you're into somebody, and he's into you, I say go for it. Get laid." Zena raised her pointer finger above her head.

"I hope that motto brings you a lifetime of happiness," I said.

"You are so naive, it hurts." Zena looked across the room at me and wrinkled her face. "What is that? What did you break?"

"It's a pickle dish," I said.

Zena began laughing. "Who in their right mind owns a pickle dish? You did your mother a favor by breaking it."

Zena could be so rude. She had a hard time understanding anybody who wasn't herself.

"Don't make fun of my mother," I said. "She's mine."

I gave Zena a powerful stare, much the same way I imagined a mother bear glares at anyone or anything approaching her cubs.

"Touché," Zena said, popping another grape into her mouth. "Hey, whatever happened to that picture of Jesus?"

Zena pointed to a bright, square patch of wall above the couch.

"It fell behind the couch," I said.

Zena rolled onto the floor and thrust her hand under the heavy beige sectional.

"I can't feel it," she said.

"Why do you care?" I asked.

"I might be an atheist, but it still seems wrong to let Jesus fall behind the couch."

I agreed and got Zena a flashlight. After several swings, her arm fully outstretched, she finally gave up.

"Do you know what I liked most about that picture?" she asked. "Jesus was blond. All that long, flowing hair. He looked Nordic. Maybe Danish. Your parents know He was Jewish, right? I mean, He was born in Bethlehem. That's in the Middle East."

"They know," I said. "My mother bought it at the mall. It went with the sofa."

Zena smiled. "But that picture didn't even look like Jesus. You get that, right?"

"Okay, so my mother likes to think of Jesus as a blond. Religion is a very personal matter. So are mothers. Let's drop it."

"Yeah. Isn't it lousy that we need mothers? What was God thinking? Hey, Tess—do you believe in God? Do you think God could be a woman?"

I didn't like engaging in philosophical discussions with Zena. She was just way too opinionated.

"Yes, I believe in God. No, I don't think He's a woman."

"God could be a woman," Zena said, setting down her bundle of grapes. "Give me one reason why God couldn't be a blond bombshell?"

Bang. Bang. Bang.

Somebody with a strong fist was knocking on the front door. But they didn't knock on the wood part, they knocked on the screen door's metal frame. It sounded like somebody was trying to shoot at us.

"I have an overnight delivery," said the UPS man. "It's for Tess Zena Crow Whistle."

Zena jumped up and ran to the door.

"I'll sign for it," she said.

I didn't understand what was happening. Was it my package? Was it hers?

"Have a nice day, Ms. Whistle," the deliveryman said.

The return address said the box was from Nevada.

"Who's it from? Is it mine? What's in it?" I asked.

"I don't think you want me to answer that," Zena said. She looked at me so hard with her gold-flecked, forest green eyes that I thought she was going to tip me over. "It has nothing to do with you," she said. "It's for that demonic beast."

I knew instantly that she was talking about the poodle. I couldn't believe that she was having bomb-making materials shipped to my house.

"This is insane," I said. "You can't do this. I don't want to be involved."

"Relax," said Zena. "People order fireworks through the mail all the time."

The package was the size of a shoe box. Zena didn't want to set it down.

"It's getting late," Zena said.

"It's four o'clock."

"I need to go home."

"Zena, you might not love that dog, but I bet its owner does. Really, you should drop this."

"The poodle's owner is of no concern to me."

"If you're that mad at it, maybe you could shave it or something," I said.

"Hair grows back. I want to erase that dog from the planet."

As she spoke, she didn't look at me. She only

looked at the box. Then, instead of rushing out the front door, she ran into the kitchen. She came back carrying a metal, rectangular cake pan.

"Do you want to borrow that?" I asked. I was a little worried that she planned to use it in the bomb assembly. My mom's name was written on it in permanent marker. It didn't seem fair to tie her to the crime.

"No," Zena said. "I just hate to see a site for worship stripped bare."

She stood on the couch and hung the metal pan on the nail intended for the picture of Jesus.

"Everybody should worship something," she said.

"Cake?" I asked. "That's so sacrilegious."

Zena smiled at me the way I imagine a fox would smile at another fox.

"Not cake. Brownies," she said. She stepped off the couch and walked to the front door. "I'll call before I go to bed."

Zena, with the package gripped to her chest, hurried out my front door, down the cement steps, and climbed into her Mercury. Before she drove off, she rolled down her window.

"Hey, Tess, do you believe in God because you believe in God, or because your parents brought you up that way?"

I didn't answer.

"They also believe in a blond Jesus," she said. "Why not believe in brownies?"

She could be so irreverent. She smiled at me, winked, and then drove home. Of course, I immediately unhung the brownie pan. I also considered pulling the nail out of the wall, but I didn't. Then it would have left a hole. I peered into the dark crack that had taken the Jesus picture. I thought about trying to fish it out, but really, that was my parents' job.

Later that night, just like she said, Zena called me before she went to sleep.

"Tess, I didn't mean to be hard on you today. Do you forgive me?" Zena asked.

"Yes," I said. First, I didn't think she was that hard on me. And second, I always forgive Zena. Then our conversation drifted to one of the things that really bonds us together, our desire to get out of Idaho.

"Once you're at UCLA, you'll be able to go to Venice Beach every day after class. I've heard there's a guy there who jumps in glass in his bare feet. Of course, if you watch him, you should leave a tip," she said. And then she talked about all the places she planned to visit in New York: the Met, Central Park, Times Square, and the Federal Reserve Bank. She went on and on. We talked about her visiting Los Angeles and shopping with me on

Melrose Avenue, and me visiting her in New York and taking the Staten Island Ferry to see the Statue of Liberty.

"The boat ride's free, you know," Zena said.

"I had no idea," I said. "Is it safe?"

"It's a short ride," she said. "But if we must, we can stand by the box of life jackets."

"I read about a ferry flipping over at least once a year," I said.

"In New York?"

"No, I think it usually happens near Bangladesh."

"Well, that's so relevant, maybe we should both wear inflatable pants." Then she started talking about taking weekend excursions to Santa Barbara and Boston. "We'll see each other so much, it'll be like we're bicoastal." And Zena was so happy when she said this that she squealed. Throughout our conversation, she didn't mention my virgin state. Or Ben. Or the bomb. Or the poodle. Or any of her other problems. I found this suspicious and alarming.

Once, a redheaded, pink-faced counselor came to our seventh-grade social studies class to discuss teenage issues. She visited the Monday after the weekend that Lane Diggers tried to burn down the school. Lane claimed it was an innocent smoking-related accident. But he never was able to explain why he'd brought a five-gallon container of gasoline, or why he'd left a note taped to the flagpole that read, "Burn, baby, burn."

The redheaded, pink-faced counselor said that when somebody's life is full of problems, that's when they go into overload, they need an outlet. I was starting to worry that Zena's outlet was making explosives. To fully communicate how dire the situation was, I must divulge several intimate details concerning Zena Crow.

First, Zena Crow confused the fact that she didn't like to wear underpants with the notion that she'd make a good anarchist. She was hardwired to buck the system, but was far too impulsive or emotional to successfully launch a coup or anything. Second, her life was a total mess. During this past summer break, everything about it had fallen apart.

It was sad, but Zena's mother, in the midst of menopause, on the fifth of July, directly following her annual Pap smear, had run off with her gynecologist. Meanwhile, in her absence, her father had begun dating their perky, big-bosomed dental hygienist—Mindy Lindy. Zena should have been crushed. But she pretended like nothing had happened.

Even though a lot of people were aware that her mother had run off to Seattle with Dr. Tong, Zena

kept telling everyone that her mother was at a Mary
Kay convention in Winnipeg, Canada, that she'd be
coming back a new woman in a pink Cadillac.

Furthermore, Mr. Crow had been seen at the
movie theater necking with Mindy Lindy. But Zena
insisted that her father, a U.S. postal carrier, was
considering a career shift into family dentistry. The
relationship between Mindy and her father, she
assured them, was strictly a fact-finding endeavor.

I knew that all this denial couldn't be good. In
anatomy and physiology we'd learned that denial
could be stored in your internal organs and cause
tumors. Okay, that's not exactly what the teacher
said, but that's the impression I was left with.

Worse still, Zena's love life had gone down like
the Titanic. Actually, her relationship plummeted
quite a bit slower than that particular ocean liner.
Her doomed union took a year to sink. Zena and her
boyfriend, Robert Bean, hit the iceberg in November
of our sophomore year. Disgusted by the presidential
election, Robert had repeatedly threatened to become
a foreign exchange student.

"Baby, don't let politics tear us apart," Zena used
to coo while running the fingers of her left hand
through his dark brown hair, and using the fingers
of her right hand to feed him Twinkies.

As a bystander, it struck me several times during

our sophomore year that their relationship was
destined to capsize. But they kept afloat. Even during
the bulk of summer. Then, without consulting her,
he signed up for study abroad and, three weeks
before school started, he flew off to Ireland. County
Cork, I think. The only postcard she received from
him told her to become an expatriate and join him
or else they should end all ties. Because her father
worked for the government, and she wasn't a fan
of either Yeats, Joyce, or rain, she opted for the
latter. Yes, hello unstable loneliness. Good-bye,
Robert Bean. As her best friend, I knew it was my
job to do something, but it wasn't like Zena had
one problem or even two. Zena Crow was facing a
tsunami of problems. And I wasn't quite sure what
to do. I mean, these weren't your average problems.
She wasn't coming unglued because of acne issues
or prom stress. Her parents had basically abdicated
their roles as guardians and she was building a
bomb. In order to kill a poodle.

These problems were as foreign to me as our
French exchange students. Plus, I'd only taken one
semester of psychology and all Mr. Biloxi had wanted
to talk about were issues related to bereavement, bed-
wetting, and body image. He also preferred it if we
called him Mr. B. In retrospect, I think he had a real
"B" hang-up. Anyway, considering the state of my

own life, and the fact that I didn't have cable, I guess I thought Zena's problems were just beyond me.

I don't like admitting this, but maybe Zena Crow wasn't the only Rocky Mountain High School junior living in denial.

Chapter 4

Two months into my junior year, I was still a virgin, Zena hadn't blown up anything, Zena's parents were still totally messed up, Ben, a voracious reader, was becoming more popular, and my mother hadn't noticed that I'd broken her pickle dish. That was the great thing about that pickle dish; it was a rarely used household item.

One Wednesday morning I woke up feeling miserable. And after a quick shower, I noticed four zits. They were juicy and painful and strategically positioned on both cheeks, my nose, and forehead. I felt like a total leper. I held back my brown bangs, popped them, dabbed them with Zit-Be-Gone cream, finished getting ready, and went to the kitchen for a piece of dry wheat toast. (I also took a good multivitamin, because, as my mother often reminded me, osteoporosis is a preventable condition.)

My mother stood at the kitchen window, watering
her windowsill-grown herbs with her right hand,
while clutching a thick black book in her left.
(I assumed it was her Bible.) I don't know how
aware she was of the fact that she was about to say
something that had the potential to ruin my day/
week/life.

"Oh, honey," she said, turning away from her
small pots of oregano. "What size shoes are those?
Are you stuffing the toes with tissue paper? They
look so big. Your feet aren't that big, are they? They
look flat. Have your arches fallen? For a man, flat
feet will keep him out of the military, but for a
woman, they're no good at all. Let me have a look
at your feet."

And so I surrendered my feet to my mother's cold
hands and scrutiny. She was shocked by the length of
my toes. The way she stretched them out one by one,
I was sort of surprised too. They looked like monkey
feet. Soon, I was upstairs, retrieving the toe-pinching
loafers.

"Your feet look half as big," she said, sounding
amazed.

So I grabbed a piece of dry wheat toast and stood
in between the screen and front door, in my tight
shoes, listening for Zena. I should have realized
that my socks were too thick, that they and my feet

were pushing the shoes to their breaking point. Regrettably, in an effort to feel better, I'd made the conscious decision to ignore my feet and pretend that after my well-formed ankles, my body stopped existing. So I didn't hear the leather groan.

Before I get into how my shoes exploded and brought Ben and me closer than ever, I should probably describe my parents. They do exist, and this story should probably reflect that.

My parents were my parents; they were not my friends. This was always the case. While I was walled up in my mother's womb, they were reading numerous books on the subject of child rearing. I think they were both reacting to my mother's mother, Grandma Cappy, and her incredibly lenient parenting style. They read countless books on child development. So when I popped out, they were absolutely ready.

I was born in Idaho. So were most of my friends. So were most of their parents. My parents were not. They were native Californians. Upon learning this fact, many of my peers leaped to the conclusion that my parents must be cool. But it's not like my parents were from Los Angeles or Santa Cruz. My parents were born and raised in Barstow, a place in California that's beachless, Republican, and dweeby. My mother, Rita, sold vitamin tonic drinks. My father,

Gil, was a nurse. They each drove a goldenrod Buick Le Sabre ten miles below the posted speed limit, even in twenty-five-mile-per-hour zones. Taking into account the earth's rotation, it was amazing we ever arrived anywhere.

I'm certain that even when my parents were young, they weren't cool. Nor were they ever going to be cool. To prevent premature aging, in addition to juicing, they slathered their arms and faces with sunscreen. They smelled like PABA and often walked around with visible lotion marks on their forearms and cheeks. Sometimes, little white globs of it got hung up in their eyebrows.

Their fear of melanoma surfaced at about the same time they became born again. So did misgivings about intersections, ground beef, and cable. Because of this, I wasted a lot of my postpubescent life looking both ways for traffic, over and over. And I didn't eat nearly enough hamburgers. And lessons I could've learned by watching television, seeing other troubled teens screw up their lives, I had to learn the hard way, on my own.

My mother once told me that the big reason we never subscribed to cable was that she was petrified that we'd somehow stumble upon pornography and the channel would freeze there, and initially we'd all be shocked, but eventually we'd become porno zombies. Because of this, I spent the best years of my life watching way too much PBS.

Yes, I loved them. And I'm sure they loved me. Happily, their strict religious views were beginning to loosen, resulting in a significant increase in my personal freedom. But at this point, they acted as though our relationship were something strictly biological with legal strings attached. Now back to Ben. His glorious butt. And my exploding shoes.

Ben was crouched down at his locker while I approached in my loafers. After clobbering him the first day with my backpack contents, I'd decided to always wait until he was finished before I approached. Also, this gave me plenty of time to stand and admire him. (Sigh.)

But that day, Ben took forever. I waited and waited. Then I waited longer. Of course, I did what all impatient waiters do. I cleared my throat. But I did this way too hard, and a clump of throat snot jumped into my mouth. So when Ben stood up and turned around, I was afraid to open my mouth for fear that I would reveal its slimy contents.

"How are you feeling?" Ben asked. "How's your blood sugar?"

I nodded. Enthusiastically.

"What's wrong?" he asked.

I shook my head.

"Is there something wrong with your voice?"

I shook my head more. Then I swallowed hard, using all of my spit to push the snot wad back down my throat.

"I'm fine," I said.

Sadly, my voice sounded like I'd swallowed a bassoon.

"Fine? Do you have a cold?" he asked.

"Yes," I croaked.

Ben was so sweet. He dug in his backpack for a throat lozenge. And when he handed it to me, there was a spark. Literally. It was an enormous buildup of static, which released itself in a powerful white zap.

"You're electric, Tess Whistle."

I stuck the lemon-flavored lozenge in my mouth.

"Thanks."

He knew my name. That's when I knew that I was on the right track to having his intelligent and attractive babies.

"I've been swamped with reading," he said. "This week I've gotten through *Leaves of Grass, Frankenstein,* and *Ethan Frome.* What did you think of *Frankenstein?* Can you believe she wrote that when she was nineteen?"

Typically, to lead into the Halloween season, *Frankenstein* was the novel imposed on junior English. I was going to read it soon. You were assigned

Leaves of Grass for sophomore English fall reading. Traditionally, seniors were given Shakespeare's *Hamlet*. But a lot of parents were in an uproar about their children being forced to read literature written by "depraved artists."

In an attempt to activate their students' interest in the material, certain teachers had spread the word that Whitman was gay, Shakespeare had probably slept around, and Mary Shelley, at sixteen, had run off with Percy, her husband-to-be, while he was still married to another woman, who later committed suicide. The school buckled under the barrage of complaints they received from concerned parents.

So senior English bumped William Shakespeare for Edith Wharton, who apparently wrote more than she had sex. I don't know why Ben was wasting his time reading *Leaves of Grass*. He wasn't a sophomore. Then again, he wasn't a junior, either, but he was in my English class. But sometimes our school mixed seniors into junior AP classes. Our school didn't have a ton of AP students.

"Tess," he repeated. "Can you believe she wrote *Frankenstein* when she was nineteen?"

The correct answer: "Why, no, I can't believe that, Ben. Mary Shelley was so talented."

The actual answer: "*Leaves of Grass.* Why are you reading that? Isn't that the poem where Walt Whitman smells his armpit?"

Ben's answer: "Yeah, Whitman smells his armpit. But I don't think that event is central to the poem."

My response: "Maybe it's not central. But it sure is memorable."

Ben's response: "You're right. I like your sense of humor."

Ben smiled at me, slammed his locker, and was just about to walk off. That's when we both heard a bizarre sound. It was a cross between a pair of pants ripping open and a fart. At first, I was mortified that he'd think I was some kind of indiscriminate farter. But there wasn't even a hint of a foul or sulfurous odor. We looked around. We were the only two people standing by the lockers. The bell was about to ring. We were going to be late.

Late or not, I was excited to be walking to class with Ben. Then I took my first step. When my feet came out of my shoes and I began nosediving in the direction of the common's bristly brown carpet,

I was certain I was going to experience a painful smack, followed by a nasty case of carpet burn. Then gravity stopped working. I hovered three inches above the carpet, suspended in air. Then I realized that Ben's arms were holding me. It was like we were ballroom dancing and he was dipping me, only instead of gracefully lowering my back to the floor, I was plunging headfirst toward it.

He tilted me upright. I blushed. Then I quickly reinserted my feet into my shoes. Ben watched as my shoe tops flapped over, hanging out like a couple of wayward tongues. I reached down and pulled the tops back, setting them on my feet, but then the sides fell open. It was as though the shoes' seams had vaporized.

"Tess, I think they're broken," Ben said.

"Oh, they'll be fine. This happens all the time," I said.

"It does?"

Ben cocked his head to one side and watched me as I attempted to tuck the leather back into place. Of course, the second I put my feet in motion, the shoes slipped off again. The bell rang. We were both late for class. Ben could have said good-bye and been gone. But he didn't. Solving my shoe problem became a collaborative effort.

"I think they're too small for your feet," he said, picking up my right loafer in his hands. The camel brown leather was stained and well worn, and my face burned red while he examined it.

"It's dead," he said with a smile, handing it back to me. "What size are you, ten?" he asked.

"Size nine," I said. But when my eyes met his, I couldn't lie. "And a half."

"Really?" he said, peering at my tan-socked feet. "My mom is a size ten, and your feet look exactly like her feet."

"Maybe I should try a ten," I said. By now, I was holding both of my worthless shoes.

"In my car, I have a pair of my mom's running shoes. She ran a half marathon last week. They were her backup pair. You can borrow them for the day," he offered. Ben reached over and gave me a hug. He laughed, grabbed my hand, and led me to the parking lot. I think he could sense that I was nervous when, as a hawk flew overhead, my muscles tightened and I ducked. I also ripped my hand out of his grasp, shielded my head with my arms, crouched down, and screamed. (Just a little.)

"It's after mice," he said, pointing to an already harvested hay field across the street. I nodded and tried to forget about the school assembly in fourth grade where they had a hawk fly around the gymnasium, circling above us, its long, deadly talons dangling below its feathered body.

When we got to his blue Chevrolet, he looked at me, laughed again, and gave me another hug. "Tess Whistle," he said, "you've got an interesting take on the world."

"My family doesn't subscribe to cable."

He laughed again. "Yeah, I try not to watch a lot of TV too. I've got a few favorites. Game shows are always cool."

"I've seen *Wheel of Fortune*," I said. That's when he really started laughing. He even grabbed his stomach.

"You kill me," he said.

"Yeah, only that wasn't a joke," I said.

But it didn't matter. All the way back to the school's front door, he laughed and laughed. It didn't even matter what I said. He said it was my delivery. Then, before he swung the door open for me, he punched me softly in the arm. I clenched my fist and considered returning the gesture, but didn't.

As we parted ways to go to class he waved good-bye to me and said, "I bet you remember this day for the rest of your life."

Chapter 5

Wearing shoes that fit my feet drastically altered my attitude. I was a much happier human being. My feet felt liberated, like they'd made it out of Communist China and were enjoying newfound democratic freedom in Portland, Oregon. (I'd never been to Portland, Oregon, but I'd always thought of it as one of freedom's major hubs.) I returned the shoes to Ben the next day, after drenching them with an antifungal powder. Of course, I didn't have a foot fungus, but it seemed like the polite thing to do.

I clomped my liberated feet around school, feeling good but probably resembling Sasquatch. It helped that Ben complimented me every morning on my shoes, even when they were the same pair. Zena didn't say anything. Zena always told the truth. And the truth was, I had very big feet. Luckily for Zena, I knew when to tell the truth and when to fudge it.

Luckier still for Zena, in addition to being a decent fudger, I was also willing to share answers. I saved her butt.

One day, Mrs. Hovel called on Zena and asked her a very specific question about last night's reading.

"Ms. Crow," she said, "In William Carlos Williams's poem 'This Is Just to Say,' who ate the plums that were in the icebox?"

Zena looked down at her desk. That's when I noticed that she didn't have any of her books. She was so bomb-obsessed that she had become a bad student. I knew she wasn't going to get into Barnard acting like this.

"Ms. Crow?"

"I think it's open to interpretation," said Zena.

"The poem clearly states who ate the plums," said Mrs. Hovel. "Have you read the poem?"

"Yes," said Zena.

"Have you forgotten who ate the plums?" she asked.

I wrote in big block letters, "HE DID." I moved the piece of paper to the edge of my desk so Zena could see it.

"No, I remember. He ate the plums. The hungry poet," said Zena.

The class laughed. I didn't know what was so funny about hunger. Then Mrs. Hovel started talking about a red wheelbarrow and white chickens and grilling us about why we thought the chickens were white. In the end, everybody agreed that William Carlos Williams had said that the chickens were white because the chickens probably were white in real life. After serious contemplation, most chickens, we thought, were either white or off-white, especially common chickens, which we felt were the variety most likely to hang out by a wheelbarrow. Mrs. Hovel seemed disappointed. Discussing the hidden meaning in colors was one of her favorite topics. White in particular.

After class I asked Zena why she hadn't done the reading. That wasn't like her at all.

"Meltdown," she said.

"Have you thought about talking to somebody?" I asked.

"I have, but I don't want to hire an accomplice. And I'm planning to saw it open on my own."

I stopped walking to my geometry class and grabbed Zena's arm.

"What are you talking about?" I asked.

"I had an accident. I melted my locker shut. I'm planning to stay after school and saw it open after everybody goes home."

"How do you melt a locker shut?" I asked.

"You don't want the details. I have a saw and a

crowbar in my car. I've got plenty of arm strength."
She pulled up her sleeve and flexed her upper arm
like she was Popeye. "I'm sure I can get it open."

Zena hugged me and walked off like it was no
big deal. I felt like I'd been punched in the stomach.
How serious was she about this bomb? Before I
could say anything dissuasive about bomb building
or dog annihilation, Zena was gone. She'd caught
me so off guard that before I could offer any friendly
counseling, I was standing by myself.

I knew Ben could tell something was wrong when
he saw me at my locker and asked, "What's wrong?"

"I'm tired," I said.

"Is it your blood sugar?" he asked.

"Could be," I said. "I think I need a Diet Coke."

"Diet Coke won't help your blood sugar. It's just
full of chemicals and caramel food coloring."

"Yeah," I said.

"What class do you have now?" he asked.

"Geometry," I said.

"East wing?" he asked.

"Yeah," I said.

"I'll walk you. Then I'll drop by and take you out
to lunch."

"Can Zena come?" I asked. "I don't want to leave
her alone."

Ben wrinkled his forehead, like he was thinking

really hard about what he was going to say. "Is Zena okay? Are you upset about Zena?" he asked.

I didn't respond. My eyes filled with tears.

"Let's go to the vending machine and get you some juice. We'll tell the office you had low blood sugar. I'm sure you can get a pass."

I was low, but I don't think my condition was related to my blood sugar. Ben inserted three quarters into the machine, and a box of apple juice tumbled to the bottom. He took my arm and walked me to the empty cafeteria. I'd have thought that the lunch ladies would have called the principal and had us removed. But everybody let us be. The smell of corn dogs and spice cake floated through the air.

"Zena is trying to build a bomb. She wants to blow up a poodle."

Ben laughed and shook his head. "I love your sense of humor."

"No," I said. "She's building a bomb. She says she wants to blow up the poodle soon."

Ben put his pointer finger to his mouth, signaling for me to be more quiet.

"You need to stop saying the word 'bomb.' You could get in trouble. Call it a doughnut. So how long has Zena been talking about the doughnut?"

I sucked on the small white straw. The sweet juice flooded my tongue and teeth. I hoped that pretending you were a diabetic couldn't somehow lead to a person actually becoming one.

"She became fixated on the doughnut after her mother ran off with her gynecologist, her father started making out with the dental hygienist, and her boyfriend fled to Ireland where he's living as an expatriate or something like that."

"Are you serious?"

"Totally," I said.

Ben and I talked all through second and third period and even into lunch. Ben bought me another box of apple juice, and my head started to ache.

"Is the poodle hers?" he asked.

"I don't know who the poodle belongs to. She doesn't say anything that will get me involved."

Ben raised his eyebrows and looked surprised.

What a dumb thing for me to say. If Zena didn't want me to be involved, she wouldn't have told me about her stupid plans to begin with.

"To be honest, I'm not sure if this is about the poodle or its owner," I said.

"What's your plan?"

"Well, I've been considering researching significant works of literature that feature dogs, especially poodles, because she's such a book lover. I figure if I can illuminate the importance of poodles at the literary level, maybe she'll change her mind."

"So once she finds out that John Steinbeck owned a poodle named Charley and took him on a road trip and wrote a book about him, she'll have some sort of epiphany, disassemble the doughnut, and become a poodle-loving freak?"

"Exactly," I said, nodding. I also wrote what he said about John Steinbeck on a napkin because Zena had loved *Of Mice and Men* and so I thought this was a good start.

"What's your other plan?" he asked.

I shrugged my shoulders. That's when we spotted Zena sitting in the back near the metal shop kids, a group that wasn't part of her regular crowd, nibbling on a mustard-slathered corn dog. When I told Ben that Zena had been a zealous vegetarian since sixth grade, both of us decided we needed to take some immediate action.

Chapter 6

When I called my mother and told her that Zena and I were staying after school, she sounded distracted.

"Drive safely," she said, hanging up before I was even finished talking. Which was not like my mother at all. First, I didn't drive. Second, she didn't even ask what time I'd be home.

It was five o'clock. The only people in the school were the wrestlers, practicing for next month's meet. I'd never seen a match before, but based on the sounds I was hearing, wrestling had to be violent. The wrestlers released grunts every time they charged each other. I also heard squeaking and slapping sounds. And when one of the boys was thrown down, his body sounded like a sack of potatoes smacking a slab of concrete.

Ben slid the crowbar in between the locker's blue door and yellow frame. The metal groaned as he forced the door open.

Inside, it looked like the paint on the walls of Zena's locker was peeling off. And there was also a strong chemical smell. Zena's books were wrapped in plastic and were unharmed.

"Your locker won't work after this," Ben said.

"I don't have much stuff. Tess, would you mind having a locker buddy?"

So began the locker buddy situation. So began evening telephone calls from Ben. So began the beginning of it all.

One week before Thanksgiving, my mother called me into her bedroom. Her bedroom looked like something out of a catalog. The blue floral wallpaper was perfectly hung. She had matched the seams with such precision that every blue bud, petal, and vining stem continued fluidly from one roll to the next.

I walked into the room and witnessed my mother looking surprisingly happy and amazingly young. When she didn't get outside enough, which was often, her skin looked gray. And not to be rude, but a splash of makeup wouldn't have killed her. Today, her lips were touched with a light peach glaze. Her eyes were rimmed with a soft brown color and shadowed with natural-looking earth tones. Her soft brown hair was held back with a pale yellow headband. And I swore I thought her eyelashes looked like they'd been brushed with a light coat of mascara.

She asked me to sit down next to her on her neatly made bed.

"This is tough," my mother started. "You know I love you. And I love your father. This is tough." She looked up at her popcorn ceiling, tears welling up in her eyes.

I wasn't sure where my mother was going with this.

"Are you leaving Dad? Are you having an affair? Are you getting a divorce!" I asked.

My mother slapped my leg and left what looked like a flour handprint on my thigh. Had she made a pie or something?

"Don't say such things! I love your father," she said. She stood up from the bed and paced back and forth. "But I need to know my purpose. I need to know who I am."

As my mother paced, I noticed that her hands looked like they were covered in chalk. The muscles in her legs looked much firmer than they usually did. After she turned forty, three years ago, her body had begun looking a tad doughy. But all this softness had somehow disappeared.

"I just got back from rock climbing," she said, setting her hands on her hips, leaving two pale hand marks on her black leggings. "I'm not who you think I am," she said, waving her arms around.

My stomach tightened. Once, on channel eight, on a daytime talk show, on an episode titled "I'm Not Who You Think I Am," I watched family members confess horrible secrets. A husband admitted to his new bride that he had seven other wives. A girl sobbed to her sister that she was sleeping with her fiancé. One mother confessed to her adopted children that she had once been a man.

"Who are you?" I asked.

"I don't know," my mother said. "But I'm not a vitamin tonic–selling, herb-growing, Idaho soccer mom!" she yelled.

I was going to point out that I hadn't played soccer since I was eight and a misfired ball had hit me so hard in the head that I'd thought I heard the phone ringing for the next two days. But I kept that comment to myself. I sat still and listened to her. It seemed like the polite thing to do.

"You are so strong, Tess. You and Harrison Q. Hart helped me see what I needed to see."

"What did I do?" I asked. (I didn't even have time to process the name Harrison Q. Hart.)

"You wore size-ten shoes. You did it," she said, taking off her sneakers and socks. She was sobbing.

I noticed that my mother's big toes curved in to

meet her smaller toes. Her baby toes had been so squished that the nails had fallen off. They looked malformed. They looked painful.

"All my life. All my life, I've squeezed my foot into a seven. No more!" She took those shoes and all of her other shoes and carried them down the hall to the front door and threw them outside. Then she joined her shoes and started throwing them across the lawn. She eventually ended up by the road, where a large irrigation canal carried water to all the hay fields farther south.

I stood on the cold November ground in my socks. The skin of my left foot could feel grass blades pushing their way in through the sock's cotton weave. I also experienced the sensation of stepping on a worm. This oozy encounter with nature made me feel sick.

"Are you okay?" I asked.

She didn't answer me. One by one she took the shoes and pitched them into the canal. She threw them with such force that when they plopped into the water, they sank. Of course, they eventually resurfaced and merrily floated along like miniature boats. Some beige. Some black. One pair of high-heeled brown shoes lodged themselves in the muddy bank. Shoe after shoe.

My mother had lost it, and I didn't know what to

do. I thought about fishing them out, but tossing out unfashionable shoes that didn't fit wasn't exactly a waste of money. And I didn't want to get that close to rushing water. And by the time I realized that I could have fished them out with a long stick and donated the shoes to a shelter, it was too late.

"Nice form," I said as she hurled the last shoe into the canal. But I don't think she heard me. She seemed very distracted and a bit off-kilter. As she watched the water continue to crawl along, she started to cry. At some point, I got past how uncomfortable I felt standing outside trampling worms beneath my socked feet and I turned my focus solely to her. I think I knew that she was having some sort of breakdown. I'd just never realized that a breakdown could be triggered by tight shoes.

Finally, I asked the question that was nestled in the back of my mind. "Who's Harrison Q. Hart?" I asked. "What did he do?"

My mother turned to look at me. Her face lit up. "I read his book, *Get Ripped: Find Your Body and Your Soul*."

Her face looked soft and hopeful, much the same way it looked when she talked about Jesus.

"A book?" I asked.

"He's a genius, Tess. He can peel a person's mind open like an onion, one layer at a time."

Had I thought much about this metaphor, I would have realized that it's possible to peel an onion into nothing but numerous, stinky, translucent layers. Until there's no onion left.

When my father came home, my mother's suitcase was already packed. He didn't say much while my mother unloaded on him about all the sacrifices she'd made throughout her whole life.

"I love you, Rita," he said. "If you need some time, take some time."

If he really loved her, I thought he'd put up more of a fight. I thought he'd run out and buy her roses or fall to his knees and beg her to stay. But the kind of love he had to give people wasn't the hyped-up overly dramatic variety. My father, the nurse, offered love quietly. I stood in the hallway as he and Mother hugged at the door. My mother's back was to me and my father's head was buried in her neck. At one point, he lifted his chin off of her shoulder and looked up at me and smiled.

I love you, too, he mouthed to me. But there was no sound, only the shape of words.

My mother left that night. She appeared to be driving faster than she'd ever driven before as she peeled out of the driveway. Her tires kicked up a large cloud of dust. It took several minutes for the air to settle. She drove her goldenrod Buick Le

Sabre south, nonstop to Utah, where she'd enrolled in a wilderness survival course. She planned to live for six weeks in the Utah desert. The brochure she left on the kitchen table showed people climbing rocks, rafting down rapids, and bungee jumping off a tall, concrete bridge. Next to the brochure was a fat, black book. It was *Get Ripped*, by Harrison Q. Hart. She'd secured a pale yellow Post-it to the cover with a note that said:

This is a life-changer.

My father stood next to me and turned the book over in his hands. I guess he wanted to read the blurbs on the back of it. But there weren't any. Instead, the back was dedicated entirely to the author's photo. His face was nearly life-size; he had thick blond hair, a solid jawline, and kind, dark eyes. He looked attractive, and resembled very much our blond Jesus now dwelling beneath the couch. Harrison's biography was printed across his neck and shoulders. He ran a survival camp in southern Utah. My father seemed to be reading that, too.

He turned the book over and set it down, pressing Harrison's face onto the table and a pile of crumbs.

"Do you think he'll be at the camp?" asked my father.

"It is named after him," I said, pointing to the name Hart Valley Ranch in the brochure.

On the refrigerator my mother had left a note that said:

Gone to get ripped and find my soul.

I always thought people went into the wilderness to lose themselves. But my mother had headed there with the opposite intention.

"She didn't take her Bible," he said, pointing to a dusty black book reclining lengthwise on the bookshelf.

I didn't say anything. I think the book had been an anniversary gift several years back. After a few more quiet moments, my father walked into the living room and unplugged the only television set in the house. He carried the heavy block to his bedroom and closed the door. Inside, I could hear him listening to *Masterpiece Theatre*. He didn't say anything to me all night.

When Ben called, I told him everything that had happened. Then I started to cry.

"You sure live an eventful life. You don't even need cable," he said. "Do you want me to come over?"

"Maybe," I said.

"I'll be there in twenty minutes."

That night, I didn't ask my father for permission to go out with Ben. I stood between the door and the screen and watched our dark driveway. While I waited, it was hard not to think about my fleeing mother. *I should have been paying closer attention,* I thought. *I should have been able to tell she was climbing rocks.* I was mad at her. And myself. Then Ben's headlights lit up my horrid night and I felt my body chill with excitement. As I darted out to his car, I thought back to Ben's prophetic words. They seemed to apply to this situation too. I opened the car door and told myself, *You're going to remember this night forever.*

Chapter 7

Don't leap to the conclusion that once my mother walked out, Tess Whistle became a loose girl. I didn't. When Ben picked me up in his Chevrolet, I didn't climb into his passenger seat, begging, "Take me now," or spring onto his lap and commence sucking face. I wasn't a bone-jumper. So far, Ben Easter was not my lover, if sex between a junior and a senior can even be called that. Our lips had never touched. Ben was a very good listener who happened to have a nice rear end.

He drove me to a pancake house, where I ordered waffles with bananas and walnuts on top and he got an asparagus scramble. Because I knew a diabetic shouldn't partake of the syrup caddy, I didn't even give it a single spin. When the waitress delivered our order, Ben frowned.

"Shouldn't you eat some protein with that? My

friend who had diabetes always had to eat protein when she ate simple carbohydrates."

I looked at my plate. Was a waffle a carbohydrate? What about the banana? "Yes, I probably should."

"Have some egg," he said, cutting me off a large corner.

And I vowed to myself to order protein from now on.

I told Ben about my mother and the shoes and Harrison Q. Hart. I told him about my father and the television. We talked more about Zena and the poodle. Ben held my hand. He let me dump out all my worries. Then he told me he was sorry.

"But I understand how your mom feels. Haven't you ever wondered what it would be like to just drop everything and go somewhere, like Guatemala?"

"No," I said. I blinked at him several times. Then I accidently peppered my waffles. The silence that followed was very awkward, so I decided to fill it. "It would require a ton of immunizations, and the bridges aren't all that safe there. I saw a documentary about it."

"Guatemalan bridges?"

"No, bridges in general. It's a worldwide epidemic. A real spandemic," I said, smiling.

"Very funny," he said, smiling. "Nobody sees the world like you."

"That's actually true. I have astigmatism in my left eye."

"What happened?" he asked.

"I got poked with a stick."

"No, really, what happened?"

"A boy named Willie Busk poked me with a stick in the eye in first grade."

"On purpose?"

"No, he was trying to shove it up my nose."

He started laughing. "I know personal injuries aren't funny, but you are such a riot. So is this clown still around?"

"No, he moved to Nebraska. He's probably graduated to pelting people with corn."

"Well, I'm sorry to hear about your astigmatism. If there's anything I can do in the future, let me know."

"Are you planning on a career in optometry?" I asked.

"No." He cut into his scramble with the side of his fork and took a huge bite. "But if we're ever in Guatemala and you need help crossing a rickety bridge or something, my hand will always be available."

I rolled my eyes. Sometimes his attempt at humor was way too corny. Then Ben lifted my hand to his lips and kissed it. That was our first kiss ever. I loved that it was just on my hand. Then Ben said that the road of life may be bumpy, but it will always take you where you need to go. Honestly, that comment was way too fortune-cookie sounding to me, but I smiled anyway. I mean, he was trying. And I'm a polite girl.

The days that followed the pancake house grew more and more stressful. Zena accidentally left a tuna fish sandwich in my locker overnight. Everything in there smelled fishy, even my folders, even my pens. This was pointed out to me every time I turned a corner. (Sophomore boys spend way too much time acting like comedians.)

Geometry was blowing my mind. I was forced to watch my lab partner saw open a defenseless frog in biology. (Puncturing them with a scalpel isn't the best idea, because those things retain a ton of fluid.) The PE teacher, Ms. Hoot, had decided that you needed to perform a flexed arm hang for thirty seconds to even pass the class. And in Spanish, we'd only leaned three phrases so far: *Me gusta. Soy de Idaho. ¿Donde esta la biblioteca?* And then there was English.

I think under different circumstances, I would have adored reading *Frankenstein*, but Mrs. Hovel became obsessed with the weather and the moon. Maybe a storm chaser or meteorologist might want to read Shelley's novel that way, but we hardly ever talked about the characters. I grew to hate the stinking moon.

Just when I started to daydream about taking the

GED and becoming legally emancipated from my parents so that I could begin a delightful life with Ben, I realized that Thanksgiving break loomed on the horizon. My father would need me. It was going to be his first wifeless holiday. I thought it would be good for us both to lean on each other. And I wanted to help him fill up the void. I was even willing to stuff the bird and boil the gizzard. Okay, I wasn't really willing to boil the gizzard.

Then came cleaning day and the big blow. Picture it: I'd just finished scouring away the soap scum patina on the bathtub and had moved on to duties related to dirty clothes. He stood in the hallway, his arms folded across his chest, and said, "I'd like to drive down and surprise your mother for Thanksgiving."

I didn't like the idea of being cooped up in a slow-moving Buick Le Sabre for three days, but because my father's heart was in the right place, I thought I should suck it up and go.

"I want to recapture the romance," he said, watching me from the hallway as I folded the last of the towels on the living room floor.

"That's going to make me feel uncomfortable," I said. In my mind, Thanksgiving, romance, and sixteen-year-old daughters didn't go together.

"I didn't plan on taking you," my father replied.

He held up a frozen dinner. It had a picture of two thick slices of turkey slathered in gravy, a square patch of mashed potatoes, a rectangle of green beans, and a corner of pudding. "Sometimes you have to make a sacrifice," my father said.

It was clear that he was telling me, with the assistance of a frozen dinner visual aid, that I was going to stay behind, to be the sacrifice.

"You're sacrificing me?" I asked. I was beginning to fold a pile of his T-shirts and underwear. I stopped.

"I know Zena's family has been going through an interesting time." He walked toward me, bringing the frozen dinner closer.

"I don't know if they'll even be having a formal meal. For fifteen years you've enjoyed fantastic Thanksgiving dinners. For your mother, for me, you need to sit this one out."

My feelings should have been hurt a lot more than they were, but because I knew that my father had gone insane, I tried not to take the upcoming abandonment too personally. And then, like a bad after-school special, two days before Thanksgiving, my father pulled out of the driveway and I stood in the front window watching him go. Rising dust clouded the air. Just like my tightly wound mother, my tightly wound father had lost it. Now, he was gone. My father ditched me, leaving fifty dollars and the numbers for the plumber (just in case), and my mother's survival camp.

I walked to the kitchen and got the brownie pan. Then I hung it up on the wall. I'm not sure why I did this, but it did make me feel slightly better. I could see my mother's Bible still nestled on the bookshelf. Seeing it lying there, so utterly unused, it reminded me of my first Game Boy, or collection of rubber stamps—things that at one time people in this area had grown to believe were essential but over time had proved to be nothing more than fads.

Thanksgiving was still two days away, but I opened the freezer and looked in on my turkey dinner. The sodium approached two thousand milligrams. As a nurse, he should have known better. I chucked the box in the trash, called Ben, and he showed up twenty minutes later with decent snacks and two movies I hadn't seen yet: *Dolphins Can Count* and *The Life Cycle of a Clam*. It turns out that when he was very young, Ben had wanted to become a marine biologist. But he was now leaning toward becoming a doctor.

Apparently, he still hadn't kicked his love of marine life. Because it was a school night, we only had time to watch one movie. Of course, I chose the film about the dolphin. Also, because my father had moved the television into my parents' room, we ended up watching it on their bed. Although, neither one of us really watched it.

That night, Ben held my hand and fed me Cheetos. When he placed the twiglike orange puffs on my tongue, sometimes he kissed my ear. The first time he did this, my body shivered. And while I was shivering, he whispered, "Lady, you look good." Then, he did the cutest thing. Just like that scene in *Lady and the Tramp*, Ben held one of the Cheetos in his mouth and he leaned in. I bit it in half. I didn't even mind that he was calling me a dog, because she was such a cute dog. I was his Lady. Our noses touched and we kissed again. I suddenly felt like I couldn't get close enough to him. Our kisses tasted like cheddar cheese, Milk Duds, and Diet Cherry 7UP. (I only consumed three-and-a-half Cheetos and one Milk Dud.)

Then things started to get steamy, and I pushed him back. The television screen was blank; the movie had finished, and neither one of us had noticed. Ben got up and flipped it to the local news. On channel eight, a reporter was talking about the dangers of heating water in your microwave oven.

"It's called superheating," he said. "And the results can be deadly."

Ben and I looked at each other.

"Have you ever heard of this?" he asked.

I shook my head no.

Then they showed the reporter wearing a white protective suit and yellow gloves. It looked like he was prepared for somebody to drop an atomic bomb on him. Then they showed him heating two cups of water in a glass bowl.

"Don't try this at home," he said.

Ben laughed. But I didn't. You could tell something big was about to happen. Then the reporter took the bowl out of the microwave and touched the hot water with a fork. There was a large explosion, and the water went everywhere—mostly on the suited reporter. Then they showed footage of several severely scarred housewives.

"This is awful," I said.

"What exactly caused this?" the reporter asked. "Heating water inside a microwave in a container that doesn't assist bubble formation. What should you do?" he asked, pointing his yellow-gloved finger in our direction. "Heat your water on a stove top and remember to handle all heated liquids with respect."

"Thanks, Bob," the news anchor said. "And stay tuned for Cautious Bob's report later tonight on how to defend yourself from a charging elk."

Ben started laughing so hard, he rolled off the bed.

"Are you going to stay for that?" I asked.

"Oh, yeah, I'm staying for that," he said.

We had to endure several boring segments about water levels and highway conditions before Cautious Bob came back. This time he was wearing a leather jacket and jeans. "Here in Idaho, just like chipmunks and bluebirds, elk are a fact of life."

I had to chuckle at this comparison.

"Here are my five tips for outsmarting a charging elk. First, never approach a bull elk during mating season."

I totally lost it. I rolled onto the floor laughing too.

"We're going to miss the other four tips," Ben said, catching his breath. He pulled me to him and kissed my neck.

"Cautious Bob is the king of obvious advice. I don't think we're missing much. Besides, it's a repeat. I saw this elk segment last year."

"Kiss me," he said.

"Now?" I asked.

"Like the candy," he said. "Now and Later."

So we kissed for a while. Then Ben abruptly stopped and tried to converse some more.

"Have you ever thought about going on a game show?" he asked.

"Sometimes you're so random," I said.

"That's always been something I've wanted to do before I die."

"Like *The Price Is Right*?"

"No," he said. "I mean, I wouldn't mind winning a car or spinning the big wheel, but I'd really like to be on *Password*."

"Isn't that a board game?" I asked.

Ben rolled on his side and propped himself up on his elbow. Then he bunched up his face and looked offended.

"*Password* is the best game show ever invented by God or man."

"You think God comes up with game shows?"

"I think He inspires men and women to achieve greatness and *Password* is definitely great. Actually, it's beyond great. *Password* won the first-ever Daytime Emmy Award for Outstanding Game Show in 1974."

I rolled onto my side too. I couldn't believe it. Ben was totally serious.

"So you've never seen it?" he asked.

"No. What's so great about it?"

He tapped my nose with his index finger. It smelled a lot like Cheetos.

"This is how you play. There are two teams and a moderator. Each team has a regular person paired with a celebrity partner. Usually, the celebrities are pretty good at word association and deductive reasoning."

"Of course," I said, trying to sound very interested.

"The moderator gives the first team a word, like

'eagle,' and only one person gets to see it. This person gives their partner a one-word clue, like 'bird.'"

"Nobody will guess 'eagle' with the clue 'bird.'"

"Right, so that person might guess 'pigeon' and be wrong, and then the other team gets to guess. The second person's clue might be 'majestic.'"

"That's actually a good clue," I said.

"But their partner might guess 'falcon.'"

"You think a falcon is majestic? I think they're cocky."

"Anyway, 'falcon' would be wrong, so it would go back to the first team and that player might give the clue 'patriotic.' And their partner might guess 'eagle' and score the point."

"We should play this game in Spanish. I would learn a ton of the vocabulary."

"We should play this game period. It's great."

"What happens if you win?"

"You advance to the Lightning Round."

"What's that?"

"More *Password!*"

"Oh. I'm surprised it got canceled."

"Well, *Password* had a long run. Losing the first host definitely hurt its chances. It got canceled in the eighties."

"How did they lose the host? Did he move to another game show?" I asked.

"No. His name was Allen Ludden. He died of

cancer."

"Well, if the host is dead, there's no way it's coming back."

"It could. And if they ever bring it back, with a different host, I'm going to try out for it. It was the best game show ever. Okay, I'm thinking of a word, and I want you to guess it. Here's the first clue: 'flames.'"

"Burger King," I said.

"No, how did you get Burger King?"

"They flame-broil their burgers. They're the only big chain hamburger joint in town that does."

"No, the word was 'fire,'" he said.

"Oh, your clue should have been 'conflagration.'"

Ben didn't say anything in response.

"Do you want to play again?" I asked.

"No," he said. "I should get going."

He kissed me good-bye, but I didn't let him pull away. We kissed again and again, until we were rolling around on the floor totally making out all over again. Ben was a real gentleman. He didn't even try to get under my shirt. And I behaved myself too. When he left that night, I gave him a long kiss and swatted him on the butt. He walked backward to his car, his lips puckered like a happy fish.

Chapter 8

The next morning, Zena picked me up for school and I told her about my father's unexpected departure.

"There's something in the water," she said.

"Really?" I said. Anytime our drinking water was under a boil watch, Zena seemed to be the first person who knew about it.

"God, Tess. I meant that it's quite a coincidence that both of our parents are acting needlessly reckless and daffy."

Zena stopped at the intersection and, instead of zipping across toward school, she sympathetically laid her hand on my knee.

"Daffy?" I asked.

She punched on the gas and sped across the highway.

"Tossing your shoes in a canal and hightailing it to a survival camp led by handsome Harrison Q. Hart does strike me as mildly eccentric."

"Yeah," I said, watching the windowless brick building grow closer and closer. "It does."

Just then, out of nowhere, a small red fox darted in front of the car. Zena slammed her foot on the brakes and jerked the wheel to miss it. My head knocked against my window.

"I'm sorry," Zena said, pulling the car back under control.

In driver's ed we'd been taught never to swerve. We'd been told to hit whatever was in the road.

"Your life is more important than a flea-ridden squirrel's," the teacher had said.

"I'm sorry," Zena repeated.

"You should've hit it," I said. I was surprised by how angry I sounded.

"It wasn't like I made a decision," she said. "It was just there. And I'm not a natural-born fox-squisher."

And for a moment, I grew hopeful. Maybe Zena wasn't a natural-born poodle-annihilator, either.

Zena pulled into the school lot and parked her car.

"I'm sorry," she said. "Next time I'll hit it."

"Don't worry about it," I said. Vehicularly speaking, it was the only close call she'd ever given me.

As we made our way up the walkway to the front door, I told Zena that if she wanted to come, Ben had invited her over to his house for Thanksgiving.

There was a long pause.

"No chance in Hell," she said.

I thought that was a bit harsh.

Then she stopped walking and dropped her backpack on the ground.

"The all-boob dental assistant, Mindy Lindy, is coming over and bringing a turkey and a four-year-old," she said.

"Boy or girl?" I asked. Without looking twice at us, a large, punctual crowd moved around us to make it inside before the warning bell.

"I always assumed that turkeys were girls, because all people are interested in is their juicy breasts."

We began moving too, making our way to my locker.

"No, is the four-year-old a boy or a girl?"

Zena shrugged and set her backpack down beneath my locker and unzipped her slim blue purse.

"Who cares?" she said, coating her lips with a pink, filmy gloss. "It's hers. And if you think I'm going to abandon an opportunity to thwart their love, you're wrong. Dead wrong." To make sure I got the point, Zena aimed her tube of lip gloss at me and simulated the sound of a gun being fired.

I stepped aside and let her into my locker.

"Okay," I said. "I hope you enjoy the meal."

"I will," said Zena, laughing. "You can bet your life on that one."

I didn't like Zena using the words "life" and "death," or making sound effects that resembled lethal weapons. It made me think of the innocent poodle, who was apparently not as sympathetic as a fox. I told Ben about this conversation less than five minutes after it was over.

"Do you want me to come over tonight?" he asked.

"Yes," I said. All day long I moved through school, thinking less about Zena and more about Ben, anxious for the day to end.

That night, I heard Ben pull into my driveway and turn off his Chevrolet. I heard his car door creak open and his footsteps grow louder as he approached my house. With my parents gone, I felt incredibly free. They were off living their daffy lives in Utah. And I was living my life right here in Idaho with Ben.

It only took twenty minutes until Ben and I were macking on my parents' bed. I always thought I would have been the kind of girl who said *slow down, no,* and *stop doing that right now.* But those reactions would've required me to engage my brain. And during this time, that wasn't really happening. That night, we didn't even bother turning the TV on. Cautious Bob could have been reporting about the proper way to protect your neck during a giraffe stampede and we wouldn't have cared.

Ben kept pushing my shirt up higher and higher.

He passed my belly button and I didn't resist. When he reached my bra line, he paused. I think he was waiting for some sort of signal, but I wasn't ready to give it.

Ben kissed my neck again and again. I inched up his shirt so I could hold on to his skin. I moaned and grabbed his back, lightly clawing him above his hips. We didn't talk. I think that's because conversation would have required thought, and like I already mentioned, we weren't really thinking.

In hindsight, I think lifting up Ben's shirt and groaning was interpreted by Ben as a sign to proceed. Soon, his hands had worked my shirt up all the way to my neck. I helped him slip it over my head. He took his own shirt off.

So there we were, shirtless, hooking up on my parents' bed, poised to exit the area known as "necking" and enter into the territory known as "petting." When Ben tried to unhook my bra, he was unsuccessful in pulling the clasp out of the loop. After three failed attempts, he simply slid the straps off my shoulders and tugged my bra down toward my stomach. Sadly, it wasn't a very attractive bra. It was padded and beige. I knew I'd have to start buying better ones, now that I would be showing somebody my underthings.

I don't know why, but the way Ben maneuvered

my bra got me thinking about more than just its lack-luster appearance. Out of nowhere, it struck me that Ben had probably failed at unhooking a bra before. Because he seemed totally prepared to execute this backup plan of slipping it off my shoulders. Then it really hit me: Ben Easter wasn't like me; he had experience.

"How much sex have you had?" I asked, pulling him close to me, pretending he was a blanket, pressing him against my naked top half.

"How much sex have I had?" he asked, trying to lift himself off of me. "Your tone implies that there's a right and a wrong answer to that one." He rolled off of me onto his back.

I pulled at my bra, resettling the straps back on my shoulders.

"I'm not a virgin," he said.

"I figured," I said, rolling onto my side, turning my back to him.

"Tess," he said. He moved close to me and kissed my back. I'd never realized how sensitive my back was. Ben's kisses were so wonderful that I seriously felt like I was melting into the sheets.

"Do you really want me to talk about how much sex I've had?" he asked. "Here, let's play *Password* again. The clue is 'bull.'"

"Crap," I said. I still didn't turn around.

"No," he said. Then he made a sound like a horse and even though I didn't want to, I laughed.

"'Bull,'" he said again.

"I'm sticking with 'crap,'" I said.

"The word was 'elk,'" he said.

"I can assure you that 'elk' would never be a word on *Password*. It's too regional. 'Moose,' maybe."

"What clue would you give for 'moose?'" he asked.

"'Bullwinkle.'"

"But I might guess Rocky."

"You'd be wrong."

Ben leaned in and kissed the back of my neck deeply. "Tess, I wasn't planning on sleeping with you. I thought we were just fooling around."

And suddenly, when he put it that way, when he said he wasn't planning on sleeping with me, when he said he thought we would just fool around, when he kept planting warm kisses on my back, I found myself rolling back over to face him and unhooking my own bra. I was lonely. This was new. I couldn't stop myself. I didn't want to stop myself. He made me so happy.

Ben and I only fooled around for another five minutes. Then, he bolted. I mean that literally. In the middle of kissing my stomach, he shot straight up and insisted that we had to stop and that he had to go—immediately. He grabbed his shirt and handed me mine. He said that he was going home to take a cold shower.

After he left, I ended up hunting around for my bra. It had somehow gotten looped over my mother's favorite lamp. I took that as a sign that I needed to be more careful, because that was a total fire hazard.

I thought taking a shower would be a good idea. I tried a cold one, but it just made my skin goose pimple. Being cold reminded me I was lonely again. A warm shower worked better. I stood in the shower's flood and held myself. After a few minutes, I was glad Ben had left.

I was surprised by what had happened. Ben and I had engaged in an activity known, at least according to health class, as "heavy petting." Until that night, I'd always considered heavy petting to be a restricted activity. Meaning, it was restricted until after I got engaged. I'd never considered Tess Whistle to be the kind of girl who would let a guy explore her naked body while still in high school. But once Ben kissed me and took my bra off, I found Tess Whistle very willing to consider it. Zena had always said that we lived in a rural community where people thought premarital sex was a sin.

"It's considered fornication," she explained to me in the seventh grade. Using a stick, she drew a picture of a woman's vagina in the dirt. Then she drew a man's penis inside of the vagina. "If we lived in a big city, sex wouldn't be a big deal. Once we hit high school, our parents would put us on the pill."

Zena had to explain what the pill was to me. It sounded magical. Zena said she was going to get on it as soon as she even started thinking about sex. "The urge is very powerful," she said. "God made it that way so we wouldn't go extinct." Of course, that was back when Zena still believed in God.

That day, in seventh grade, Zena made me fearful of the urge. Like it was something I'd have absolutely no control over. Like it was as bad as a demonic possession. After this talk, for three nights in a row I dreamed that a giant white pill was chasing me down a grassy hill, trying to squish me under its chalky side. Right as the pill was overtaking me, as its shadow blocked out the sun, I'd wake up, sweating, deeply in need of a glass of water.

I remember wondering if my mother took the pill. Did she keep it hidden away in her medicine cabinet? I bet she did. I was an only child. She had to use some sort of birth control. I remember wondering all kinds of questions about sex and the pill. When had my mother first had sex? Had she waited for a ring? And I remember thinking that these were questions Tess Whistle should not, would not, and could not ever ask.

Chapter 9

I didn't spend too much time getting dolled up for Thanksgiving dinner at Ben's. He'd said that it was a very informal affair, and because I was totally falling in love with him, I took him at his word.

It wasn't until I was seated at the Easters' large rectangular table, watching steam rise off of the numerous bowls and platters, that I realized I should have offered to bring something.

"I should have brought a dish," I said to Ben's mother, who sat across from me. "I make good beans."

Ben's mother smiled. She had a pretty, round face that held many attractive and symmetrical features: blue eyes, thin nose, high cheekbones, and plump lips. Long blond hair cascaded over her shoulders, parting like a soft curtain, showcasing her well-set collarbones and ample bustline. She was also incredibly slim. I guess running half marathons has that result on a body.

"Tess, we have too much as it is. Enjoy yourself."

I got the impression that she wasn't playing any head games with me; she meant what she said. Ben reached over and touched my leg. I was happy that we hadn't gone any further and done anything below the belt. If we had, I would have felt so self-conscious in front of his family. Even though it was clear to me that everyone in attendance had already had sex. They were old and married. Except for the gardener. He was single. But he couldn't have been a virgin because he looked like he was at least thirty. *No man could hold out for that long,* I thought. I smiled at all the unfamiliar faces around the table. Ben let go of my leg and picked up his fork.

"Looks good," he said. "We should dig in."

Nobody offered to say a prayer. Where I came from, grace was always said over meals that fell on major holidays, even Labor Day and Earth Day. When I noticed that I was the only person with a bowed head, I snapped it back up. Ben looked at me with a worried expression. Then he poured me a glass of apple juice. I remember wondering how much longer I could pretend to be a diabetic. I figured at least six more years, until I was out of college, until our first baby was on the way.

The following people were present for Tess Whistle's sixteenth Thanksgiving dinner: me (the only virgin at the table), Ben, Ben's mother, Ben's father, Uncle Sam, Aunt Charma, Grandmother Nutt, Grandfather Nutt, and John the gardener.

The important thing about this meal was that it made me feel a lot better about the emotional health of myself and my family. Yes, we had some serious problems that most likely would require years of therapy, but so did a lot of people. And I mean a lot.

BEN'S FATHER: "Look at that incredible bird."

UNCLE SAM: "It's genetically altered. That's why it has such big breasts."

AUNT CHARMA: "He's not kidding. Tess, have you ever heard of the annual turkey pardon?" (I had not, so I shook my head no.)

UNCLE SAM: "Every year the president of the United States pardons a turkey so it won't get sent to the chopping block. He also pardons a runner-up."

BEN'S MOM: "Will this story make us lose our appetite for turkey?"

AUNT CHARMA: "Shhh. For people who respect animals, this is an important thing to know."

UNCLE SAM: "Every year the media shows up and the president liberates a bird. They lead you to believe that the bird lives a happy life on a farm somewhere."

BEN'S FATHER: "Who leads us to believe that?"

AUNT CHARMA: "The media and the White House work in collusion!"

BEN: "What happens to the bird? Does the White House or the media eat it?"

UNCLE SAM: "Don't get smart. The turkey is sentenced to live on Kidwell Farm, in Herndon, Virginia."

AUNT CHARMA: "It's part of Fairfax County's Frying Pan Park."

BEN'S MOM: "Dinner's cooling down. We should eat."

AUNT CHARMA: "He's almost finished."

UNCLE SAM: "Your aunt and I went to visit one of those pardoned turkeys."

BEN: "Why?"

AUNT CHARMA: "It seemed like the American thing to do. We eat them every year."

GARDENER: "Pardoned turkeys?"

UNCLE SAM: "No, turkeys in general. Nobody is allowed to eat the presidentially pardoned turkeys."

AUNT CHARMA: "Get to the part where they die."

BEN'S MOM: "I'm going to have to reheat the gravy."

AUNT CHARMA: "He's almost done."

UNCLE SAM: "We went to visit the pardoned turkeys and they were all dead. Why? Because they're genetically altered to grow so fast and big that they can't fly or sustain a meaningful turkey life."

AUNT CHARMA: "They can't even reproduce without artificial insemination."

GRANDMA NUTT: "Think of all the couples in the world who want to have children but can't. And we're inseminating turkeys."

GRANDPA NUTT: "Well, the couples want babies, not turkeys."

GARDENER: "I shot a wild turkey once. It was quick."

UNCLE SAM: "In the wild, a real turkey can fly fifty miles per hour. That's as fast as an Olympic runner."

AUNT CHARMA: "When we went to pet the pardoned turkeys, we found empty cage after empty cage. Why? Heart attacks."

UNCLE SAM: "None of them stood a chance."

AUNT CHARMA: "Commercial turkeys live horrible lives. Crammed into cages. Never really allowed to be turkeys at all."

Mrs. Easter looked like she was about to pass out. She forcefully began passing the cranberry sauce, followed by the biscuits, gravy, and mashed potatoes. Nobody else talked about the miserable lives of turkeys.

GRANDPA NUTT: "Damn good bird."

GRANDMA NUTT: "Meat doesn't taste mutated at all."

GARDENER JOHN: "Fastest bird I ever shot."

And one hour later, dinner was over and the photo albums came out. I would have been mortified if my parents had shown pictures of me topless, covered in tapioca pudding, wearing a diaper. But Ben didn't seem to mind. Things went swimmingly until he turned to the pictures of the family vacation they'd taken in Mazatlán, Mexico.

I wasn't quite prepared for the torrent of personal information unleashed by the Nutts. Naturally, I'd been expecting that dinner would be followed by pie.

Even though Sheila was tucked into the background, Grandma Nutt noticed her right away. I think it was because Sheila was topless and had a coconut shell decorated with a bright pink umbrella tipped to her mouth. It was the sort of thing that caught your eye. Apparently, years ago, Mr. And Mrs. Nutt had gone through a rough patch.

"Impudent strumpet!" Grandma Nutt huffed.

"Let sleeping dogs lie," said Ben's father, trying to make peace and turn the page.

"She wasn't a strumpet or a dog. Sheila Stadler was a dang talented poet and a fine fire-eater," Grandpa Nutt said.

Sheila Stadler was a name I'd heard before. All through fifth grade, she'd been Zena's idol.

Sheila was famous for performing her feminist monologues in playhouses throughout southeast Idaho and southwest Montana. She'd open by baring both breasts and close by lighting her tongue on fire. Sadly, two years ago, during our ninth-grade year, while crossing the Teton Pass, Sheila had struck a moose. Neither survived. People never could figure out what a moose was doing climbing up that pass.

Grandma Nutt turned bright red. She stood up and grabbed a thick phone book, the kind that offers both yellow and white pages, from the credenza. Then she tossed it hard in Grandpa Nutt's direction and sat back down.

The book flapped across the room like a fat bird incapable of flight. Grandpa Nutt lifted his arm and blocked its intended target: his bald noggin.

"This is exactly why I left you," he said. "I'm a lover, not a fighter."

"Love this!" Grandma Nutt yelled. She stood up again and grabbed the basket of wheat rolls from the table. I made a mental note that it must be easier to pelt objects short distances from a standing rather than a sitting position. She swung hard, pitching six, aiming below the belt. "Animals have more loyalty than you. Swans mate for life!"

I'd never seen adults fight using phone books and food before. The most aggressive thing my parents had ever done was slam a cupboard door. Ben looked embarrassed. His mother looked mortified. His father looked uncomfortable but somewhat engaged in the argument. The gardener kept looking at the photos of the topless woman.

"You and this swan business. I've looked it up. In the wild, a mute swan only lives for seven years, a trumpeter for twelve. I was loyal to you for twenty-seven years. I was more loyal than two swans. Until *that* day."

"It's just like you to bring up *that* day," Grandma Nutt roared. She ran out of rolls and lugged a piece of fruitcake at his head.

"Helen Cleopatra Nutt, do you deny that I caught you without your wedding ring in the arms of Ed Boot?" In a defensive move, Grandpa Nutt had positioned a throw pillow over his genital area.

"Ed Boot was consoling me," she said. Her skin looked blotchy, and she was tearing up. "And I'd taken the ring off so I wouldn't muck it up." She sat down, sobbing. I stayed seated with Ben on the couch and tried to pretend that I was watching a zany sitcom on TV.

"A wedding ring should never be taken off," said Grandpa Nutt. He lifted his left hand for everyone to see and pointed to his gold band.

Grandma Nutt blew her nose and kept talking.

"Before getting my first bikini wax, I took off my ring and put it in my purse. Then I tied Winky to a parking meter and went inside. When I came out, Winky was gone. Ed was there and he consoled me. There was no hanky-panky involved."

Ben's mother buried her face in her hands. Until that moment, I'd never thought of having my bikini area waxed.

"I've never understood how you could lose a dog. And it's tough for me to believe that a woman seeking a bikini wax without her wedding ring isn't somehow looking for hanky-panky."

"I got my bikini line waxed so I could go to Mazatlán, but you took the strumpet instead," she snapped. "And I lost the dog because I tied him to a parking meter. When I came back, the leash was cut and he was gone. Who knew a wax took that long?"

Grandma Nutt was sobbing. Grandpa Nutt ran to her side, which is what I was hoping he'd do. It was obvious that she was telling the truth. It was equally obvious that he believed her. Hence, the entire brouhaha was about to end happily, as it should, with a public display of forgiveness.

"I never should have taken Sheila to Mazatlán. Nothing happened. It was very spiteful of me," he said. "You have always been my true love."

"I'm so sorry I lost Winky," she said. "I should

have known somebody would want a border collie. After that day, I never took my ring off again."

They hugged and kissed. Meanwhile, Ben's mother pulled the photos of Sheila out of the album and set the newly edited, fat book on my lap. She tossed the objectionable pictures in the trash, but I saw the gardener fish them out and slide them into his coat pocket. This bugged me. Why was this guy even here? But I have to admit that I felt bad for him. It must be awful to reach thirty and not have found your true love.

Grandma Nutt and Grandpa Nutt were consoling each other so much that Ben whispered to me that they should just get a room. I thought it was sweet. (A lot of people think it's gross when the elderly suck face. I think it's part of nature.)

"We can look at the album another time," Ben said, wrapping an arm around me.

I'd just gotten to what looked like either his second- or third-grade pictures. Ben's smile was marked by the protrusion of an enormous pair of donkey teeth. I wanted to see more. I turned the page again. I was shocked to see pictures of Ben in a hospital bed. Pictures of Ben without hair.

"What's this?" I asked.

I think I knew that these were pictures documenting an illness; I think I even suspected cancer. But I wouldn't admit this to myself.

"When I was in third grade, when I was eight, I was diagnosed with leukemia. I'm in remission," he said. He wasn't smiling anymore, and his arm had relaxed. He wasn't holding me. He stared at the pictures.

"Why didn't you tell me sooner?" I asked. I set my hand on his knee and squeezed.

"I don't like to talk about it," he said. "You don't tell people about your diabetes. It's the same thing. I don't want people to see me as different. I don't want people to feel sorry for me."

I buried my head in his shoulder and whispered that I understood. At that moment, I convinced myself that I really was a diabetic, concealing my illness so people wouldn't pity me.

When Ben's mom brought out thick wedges of pumpkin pie topped with large dollops of whipped cream, Thanksgiving started to feel more normal. Grandpa and Grandma Nutt had taken the public displays of affection down a notch and were simply holding hands. Charma and Sam had fallen asleep in front of the television. The gardener had left, he claimed, to trim a topiary. And Ben's father was asking me about my Spanish class. I didn't even realize that the Easters' phone had rung.

"Tess," said Ben's mom. "It's for you."

I smiled at everyone and took the receiver. I knew

it was Zena because in addition to being my sole friend, she was also the only human being who knew I was at Ben's.

"You said you wanted advance warning," said Zena. "I'm blowing up the poodle in fifteen minutes."

It was very difficult, but I needed to act normal. I also needed to figure out a way to stop Zena from blowing up the dog. But I wasn't sure how to do that, so I decided to unleash a load of positive poodle trivia.

"John Steinbeck had a poodle named Charley and they rode cross-country together and he wrote a fantastic book about it," I said quietly into the phone. "Winston Churchill also owned a poodle. He named it Rufus."

"Big whoop," Zena said.

"Marilyn Monroe was given a poodle by Frank Sinatra. History is peppered with interesting poodle owners." Zena didn't say anything in response, so I continued. "After the Scottish border collie, the poodle is documented as the smartest breed in the world. And poodles don't shed, which is a boon for allergy sufferers. Plus, they're great swimmers."

"The poodle will be confettied in fourteen minutes," Zena said.

I pulled out my last tidbit. "Strawberry Shortcake's friend Crêpe Suzette had a pet poodle named Éclair."

"I've always felt crème-filled pastries were over-rated. The poodle is history."

"Come on, Zena, you believe in life after death. Don't you think that poodle has a soul?"

"It's not like I'm taking out a Saint Bernard," she said.

The next thing I heard was a click followed by a dial tone. I hung up the phone. I kept grinning.

"It looks like I have to go," I said.

Everybody who was awake groaned.

"Are you sure you can't stay?" asked Mrs. Easter.

"I'm positive," I said. "I have to help a friend."

When I said this, I sounded really confident and smiled. This was the first time I'd realized that lying doesn't have to be limited to words. My confidence and smile were absolute lies too. Because when it came to helping Zena, I was scared out of my pants and had no idea what I was supposed to do.

Chapter 10

Nobody liked the idea of me leaving without eating a piece of pie. Ben's mom had even made a low-sugar apple pie for me. But when your best friend is on the verge of blowing up a poodle, there's really no time for dessert.

"I'm sorry I can't stay," I said.

"I'll drive you," Ben said.

"What does your friend need?" asked Ben's mom.

"My friend is making a doughnut and has run into problems."

Ben caught the hidden meaning right away.

"Oh, my God," he said. "She seriously made the doughnut?"

"Did she make them out of potatoes?" asked Grandma Nutt. "I know it sounds ridiculous, but they're the very best kind. Moist as Hawaii."

"When will the doughnut be ready?" Ben asked.

"Less than fifteen minutes," I said.

"Goodness, I've never heard of such a recipe. You'll burn a doughnut to charcoal if you fry it that long," said Grandma Nutt.

"I think she's still in the dough-raising phase," I said.

Ben and I threw our jackets on and raced out to his car.

"I hope your family doesn't think I'm rude," I said.

Ben opened his car door and paused.

"If your best friend blows up a poodle, who knows what they'll think."

Ben didn't even have time to put the car in reverse before his mother ran out, holding the phone receiver above her head.

"Tess! Tess!" she yelled.

"Maybe Zena changed her mind," said Ben.

I thought that was unlikely. The Zena I had just spoken with on the phone was going to blow a poodle to smithereens in fifteen minutes. I took the phone and listened to the woman on the other end. It took a few seconds before I realized it was my mother.

"Zena gave me this number. I hope it's okay that I called. Your father coming was a lovely surprise. He and Harrison have made a true connection. Looks like your father wants to stay. He can't hike enough. Your grandmother is flying in tomorrow. You should take a cab and meet her at the airport. Use the money your father left you."

"How long will you two be gone?" I asked.

"Three more weeks for me. Your father is considering staying the whole six. It truly is a life-altering experience."

My mother had lost touch with reality. This was far more serious than her born-again phase. She was so far gone that she didn't realize how stupid and illegal it was for a mother to abandon her child, especially over the holidays, life-altering experience or not.

"Will you be back for Christmas?" I asked.

"Of course," she said. "Oh. Oh," she squealed. "Jackie Puffkin is almost to the top of the rock wall for her first time ever. God speed! Rock on! Dynamite!"

My mother was screaming so loudly that I had to hold the phone away from my ear. Ben wrinkled his face with concern.

"I've got to go. Your grandmother's flight lands at noon. She's flying from Chicago to Salt Lake, Salt Lake to Idaho Falls. She'll be tired. Help her take her shoes off. And don't let her spend too much money. I love you."

Thunderous applause erupted in the background. Jackie Puffkin must have reached the top of that wall. I handed Ben's mother their phone.

"Is everything okay?" she asked.

"Time will tell," I said.

"We've got to get to the doughnut before it's too late," he said.

There it was. One minute earlier, my best friend had called me because she needed me and I was off to help her, thinking, *Zena, Zena, Zena.* But then my mother threw me a curveball and got me thinking about all my own problems again. It's so hard to be a good friend when your life is crumbling like a stale cookie all around you.

Ben's mother waved good-bye as Ben sped his Chevrolet backward down the drive and then flipped around and punched on the gas.

When we rolled up to Zena's house, we could hear people screaming inside.

"Not my poodle!"

"Zena, you've snapped!"

"Once I marry your father, I'm sending you to the loony bin!"

"Kiss your pooch good-bye!"

Clearly, people were extremely upset. Ben acted very brave. He didn't even knock. He stormed through the front door and yelled, "Where's Zena? Where's the poodle?"

It was quite obvious where the poodle was. I was surprised that he'd bothered asking that question.

A large white standard poodle stood right beside a young crying girl. The poodle's fluffy head was taller than she was. In fact, the poodle's fluffy head came up to my bra.

Ben, still stuck in superhero mode, scooped the large dog up in his arms.

"I was expecting it to be a miniature or toy poodle," he said, straining under the dog's fluff and weight.

"What are you doing?" said Mr. Crow. "Put Madonna down."

Ben looked confused.

"I'm saving the poodle," said Ben.

"Not that poodle," said the girl. "That poodle." She pointed behind us, outside.

Ben and I both followed the aim of the girl's finger. There, in the Crows' backyard, Zena held a small pink poodle above her head. Dozens of bottle rockets were strapped to the poodle's soft body. We were too late. The dog was motionless. It must have realized its upcoming tragic fate. The dog was silent. Was it scared to death? No. It was a stuffed animal.

Chapter 11

Ben set the big poodle down beside the young girl and rushed out to the backyard. He was determined to save a dog's life.

"Back away, Easter," Zena yelled. "I've lit the fuse."

Small orange sparks popped near the pom-pom at the end of the poodle's tail. Zena shook the toy dog above her head, and Ben stayed put.

"Did you ever think of buying a second poodle?" Zena screamed. "One for me?"

Mr. Crow walked through the opened sliding-glass door onto the backyard.

"You're not a little girl anymore," he said. "I didn't know you wanted a poodle."

"If you buy one for Cindy, you should buy one for me."

The fuse continued to burn, like a disappearing worm.

"Snuff out the fuse!" I yelled.

Zena glared at me.

"I thought you were on my side," she screamed. Her face reddened. Her eyes narrowed. "This poodle is history."

With that, Zena threw the dog a good twenty feet into the air. The fabric began breaking apart when the bottle rockets shot away from the animal. Then, a large explosion erupted out of the poodle's center. Bits of flaming cotton batting drifted down onto the grass.

"My poodle!" yelled Cindy, racing into the backyard.

Mindy Lindy chased after her daughter. Mr. Crow tackled Zena and held her to the ground.

"This is very serious," he said.

"Do I look like I'm laughing?" asked Zena.

Zena and her father rolled around on the grass as he tried to wrestle a pack of matches out of her tightly closed left hand.

"Zena's mean," cried the girl. "She killed Bobo."

"I'll buy you a better Bobo," said Mindy, pulling her daughter to her overflowing bosom.

"I want that Bobo," Cindy said, pointing to the poodle scraps littering the lawn. "That Bobo was the best Bobo ever."

Mindy kissed the crown of her daughter's head over and over.

"I'll buy you a Bobo that barks and does tricks," she said.

"That Bobo was my Bobo," she wailed, collapsing on the lawn. At this point, everybody, except for me and Ben, was on the cold, November ground. The damage was done. There was nothing I could do now. I wasn't interested in getting my butt wet, so Ben and I made our way to the porch and leaned against a brick retaining wall.

"What can I do to make you happy?" Mindy asked, rolling her daughter onto her back, brushing her hair out of her tear-stained face. Cindy was so worked up that she was unable to stop her tantrum. Her body shuddered. She coughed. Snot rolled freely out of her pink nose, spilling onto her little, trembling lips.

"Blow up Zena," Cindy stuttered. "Blow her up."

Mindy pulled her convulsing daughter into her arms.

"It's against the law to blow up people," she said. "Even nasty ones."

"I want my Bobo," Cindy screamed, kicking her legs and swinging her arms.

By this point, Mr. Crow had separated Zena from her pack of matches. I'm not sure why this was so important to him. I guess it made him feel like he'd gained the upper hand. Mr. Crow led Zena over to Cindy. He held Zena by the scruff of her neck and when they arrived at the feet of Cindy, he squeezed the back of Zena's neck hard, forcing her mouth open.

"Say you're sorry," he said.

And then, like she was a ventriloquist's dummy, Zena apologized.

"Blow her up!" Cindy cried.

"Cindy, I can't blow up my daughter."

"Do it now!"

After spending five minutes watching Cindy Lindy, Ben and I totally understood why Zena had to blow up her poodle.

"Maybe we should blow up Zena," Mindy said, raising her eyebrows. "P-R-E-T-E-N-D." She spelled the word so Cindy wouldn't catch on.

"No," said Mr. Crow.

Mindy squinted her eyes into angry slits and aimed her gaze at Mr. Crow.

Ben and I held hands and tried to stay out of it.

"You can't blow me up," said Zena. "It's totally against the law."

"Tess, can you keep an eye on Cindy?" asked Mr. Crow.

I nodded that I would.

"Traitor," Zena spat at me as Mr. Crow led her into the house.

I was shocked when Zena called me that. I turned to Ben.

"Do you think I'm a traitor?" I asked. I stabbed him in the chest with my pointer finger. "I sure don't feel like Benedict Arnold. Okay, so I guess I haven't behaved like a perfect George Washington or a Paul Revere, but Benedict Arnold?"

"Why are we suddenly trapped in the Revolutionary War? Did I miss something?"

"I mean, what was I supposed to do?" I asked.

"She's just upset," Ben said.

"Okay, so maybe I've been a little overly focused on my own problems."

Ben didn't say anything.

"So you think that?" I asked.

"Nobody's perfect," he said. "We all make mistakes."

"You think this is my fault?" I poked him in the chest again. "I tried to talk her out of it. She was so determined."

"I know. She's a regular Ethan Allen."

"This is serious," I said.

"I know it is," he said. "I'm trying to keep it bearable."

Zena, Mr. Crow, and Mindy were gone about five minutes. Then Mindy, smiling, reentered the backyard. Cindy was sitting upright, collecting pieces of her charred Bobo that were within arm's reach.

"You've won," she cooed to her daughter. "He's in the bathroom blowing up Zena."

"What?" I cried.

"P-R-E-T-E-N-D," Cindy mouthed to me. She also handed me a folded-up piece of paper. "It's a letter from Zena."

As Ben and I left the backyard, Cindy danced and hopped wildly on the grass. Clearly, she was destined to grow up to be a horrible human being.

"That was so morbid," Ben said, taking my hand and leading me back to his car.

I held the note. I didn't want to open it.

"You should read it," he said.

"I can't," I said. Tears rolled down my cheeks.

"It will get better," he said.

"I guess I didn't realize things were this bad."

He opened the car door for me.

"How could you miss it?" he asked.

I sat down and buckled my seat belt. "I don't know."

"When I wasn't around, didn't you talk about it with her?"

"No," I said.

Ben walked around to his side of the car and climbed in.

"Why not?" he asked.

"Lately, we just haven't been deep like that."

"She's your best friend."

"Well, there's been a lot of distance since Robert Bean. Guys change the whole girl dynamic."

Ben didn't say anything.

"I really let her down. God, that woman is horrid. And did you get a load of that kid?"

He nodded. Ben didn't answer me. We drove in silence back toward my house. As the wind blew over the car, whistling, I pretended that it was singing to me. Sadly, the wind didn't take requests. It sang about tragedies of the worst kind: dissolving friendships, cancer, affairs, explosions, abandonment.

"I have to pick up my grandma at the airport tomorrow at noon," I said.

"I didn't know your grandma was visiting," he said.

"The state frowns on the idea of letting sixteen-year-olds raise themselves," I said.

"Tess Whistle, do you know what I like about you?"

"I'm good at *Password*," I said.

"No, that's not it. You're deep and funny. It's a great combo. Like tacos and enchiladas."

He licked his lips and rubbed his stomach like he was hungry. I know he was trying to cheer me up, but it sort of felt like he was insulting me. It's hard to take being compared to Mexican food as a compliment. I mean, it's totally starchy and gives you gas.

Ben turned into my driveway and shut off the car. He put his arm around me and asked if he could come in. He pressed his lips to my ear and blew a kiss inside of it. I jerked myself out of his arms.

"Don't blow in my ear," I said.

"I thought you liked it when I kissed your ears."

"Kiss all you want, but please don't blow," I said.

"Do you want me to leave?" he asked.

I didn't want Ben to go. I didn't want to be all by myself thinking about Zena and the day's events. I couldn't. For me, today had been just too heartbreaking.

"I want you to come in," I said, rubbing my hand across his upper thigh. "I want you to stay with me until I fall asleep."

"Okay," he said.

Chapter 12

The next morning, I woke up alone at the crack of dawn and didn't like how it felt. I rolled over to look at the side of my bed where Ben belonged, where he had spooned me until I fell asleep. The outline of his body dented the top of my bedspread. I ran my hand over the flattened area. Even though it would have been unlikely, because Ben had vacated my bed several hours ago, I expected to feel his body's warmth. But the depression that bordered my body was cool to the touch. Absence doesn't always make the heart grow fonder. Sometimes, it just reminds you that you're incredibly lonely. So I called him.

"Come now," I said.

"Did your grandma catch an earlier flight?" he asked.

I had woken him up. I could hear him yawning. For a second, I considered lying to him.

"No. My big empty house is making me sad."

He didn't put up an argument. I rushed to change my clothes and primp. When Ben arrived, I gave him a deep, full-frontal hug and ran my fingers through his hair.

"You feel so good," I said.

I didn't want to think about yesterday. I wasn't in the mood to process the cataclysmic turn Zena's life had taken, and Ben wasn't in the mood to fool around. This was a first.

"Let's take a nap," he said.

I'm not sure why we decided to spoon in my parents' bed, but we did. I folded myself against his body and held him from behind. I should have asked him about his leukemia. I should have talked to him about why he moved to Idaho from Michigan. But all I wanted to do was touch him.

I ran my fingers through Ben's hair and nibbled on his neck. He was unresponsive.

"I'm tired," he said.

I couldn't believe he said that.

"I bet you're the only guy your age not interested in fooling around," I said. "Especially in the morning."

Ben rolled onto his side and faced me. He tapped his pointer finger on my nose.

"I'm very interested in it," he said. "But I'm taking you to pick up your grandmother in an hour.

We don't want to show up smelling like we've been fooling around."

"Fooling around doesn't leave a smell," I said, reaching my hand under his shirt and crawling my fingers up his chest.

"It definitely does," he said. He pulled my hand out from under his shirt and kissed it. "Have you read Zena's letter?"

I shook my head no.

"Why don't you want to read it?" he asked.

"She thinks I'm a traitor," I said. "She's very articulate. She might actually convince me that I am one."

"Maybe that's not what the note is about," he said.

"I'll call her later," I said.

"Oh," he said in a very depressed voice.

"What's wrong?" I asked.

Ben brought his finger back to my nose and resumed tapping.

"I'm worried that they might send her somewhere," he said. "Parents perceive bomb building as a precursor to other violent behavior."

"No," I said. "Not Zena."

"I know," he said. "But you need to consider that her father might send her away somewhere."

Apparently, Zena and Ben are both clairvoyant, because when I hopped off the bed and retrieved the letter, Zena had written about her father's decision to send her to Arizona to live with her aunt. Ben still thought she had been committed, and that her father had "told" her she was going to visit her aunt so she would voluntarily board the plane. We had quite an argument about this. Then he admitted that he'd just finished reading *The Bell Jar* by Sylvia Plath, and that the novel might be influencing some of his opinions.

The following is Zena's letter:

I'm writing this letter while sitting on the toilet. My father is standing next to me. He wants me to tell you that he didn't blow me up. I told him that because you aren't retarded, you already know that. Tess, my father thinks that I have emotional problems. He's sending me to Arizona to live with my aunt, who is a licensed therapist. I don't know how long I'll live there. But my dad says I can use the phone. He also thinks that my mother will come and visit. I guess this has been in the works for a while. I'll call you. Maybe you can visit too. I know you're not a traitor. (I'm writing this note under extreme duress.) Love, Zena.

Zena's letter put me in tears. Ben held me. He kissed me over and over again and told me it was going to be okay. He held me for a long time. Then it was time to go.

When Ben stepped away from me to put his shoes on, I lost my balance and almost toppled over. He went downstairs and got me some juice. Really, I think my tippy state was a sign. I was supposed to see how much I was relying on Ben. I was supposed to realize that you can't depend on another person to provide your own balance.

But I didn't see any of that and I drank the juice and the two of us went off to pick my grandma up at the airport. I hoped that she wasn't wearing tons of gardenia perfume and that she'd stopped wearing curly red wigs. Why my grandmother, a recent winner of the Illinois State Lottery, wanted to smell like an overripe flower and look like an elderly version of Little Orphan Annie was beyond me.

My grandma won the jackpot two weeks after my grandpa had experienced a massive stroke and died. Several weeks after both events, my grandma mailed us two pictures. The first was of her carrying an enormous cardboard check with her share of the winnings, $1,900,000, printed on the front. On the back she'd scribbled, "The Lord Giveth." The second photograph had been taken of all of us at my grandpa's funeral in Rockland. We were dressed in black, barely smiling, and on its back she'd written, "And the Lord taketh away." My parents said that death brings people closer to God. At first, I took that to mean that the dead person was brought closer to God, which seemed grim. But I think that they actually meant the people who were still alive. Other than these scribbles, I hadn't detected any faith shift in my grandma.

Luckily, she didn't emit a strong floral odor, nor did she come wearing outrageous hair. She descended on the escalator looking like a class act. She wore a powder blue suit, spiffy high heels, and her hair was a newly lightened, straw-colored blond. She walked right up to me and Ben and kissed up both, leaving lip marks on our cheeks.

"He your boy?" asked my grandma.

"I'm Ben Easter," he said, shaking her hand. "Can I help you with your luggage?"

"No," she said. "I didn't bring any. No time to pack."

"You can borrow some of Mom's clothes," I said.

"Dear God, I wouldn't dream of it!" She gasped. "Do I look like a beige-addicted Westerner?"

"No, you don't," said Ben, smiling big.

"We'll shop. Today's the biggest shopping day of the year. We'll hit all the sales." My grandmother winked at me and then nodded her head to the door. "Let's blow this joint."

Ben rubbed my back as we walked out to his car. My grandma insisted on folding herself down and squeezing into the backseat.

"At my age, bending is a good habit to foster," she said.

We bumped along for about four seconds before she started asking questions.

"How's Zena?"

"She's been sent to live with her aunt," I said.

"She's been institutionalized," Ben added.

"She always had a dangerous combination of intelligence, spunk, and spine. Bless her soul." She reached around from the backseat and pet my head.

"She's not going to an institution. She's going to Arizona. Her aunt is a therapist. I might be able to visit her," I said.

"Dear God, I wouldn't," she said. "I've toured two loony bins. Both times depressed the hell out of me. I started to wonder, who's crazy, me or them?" My grandma reached in her purse and pulled out a cigarette. She lit it and puffed away.

"Uh. This is a nonsmoking vehicle," Ben said.

"I thought you quit," I said.

"My therapist says I have an oral fixation." She crushed her cigarette into the shiny metal pot of an unused ashtray. "Besides, I only get the urge when I'm traveling over forty miles per hour."

Ben slowed the car down.

"I also get the urge when I'm at the zoo," she said.

"Something about watching caged animals causes me great distress."

It wasn't until we pulled up in my driveway that I realized it was snowing. Puffy flakes were beginning to form a thin sheet of white on the lawn. Ben didn't come inside.

"I'll let the two of you get reacquainted," he said. "And shop."

"You're a catch," she said, squeezing a wad of fat on his cheek.

When we got inside, all I wanted to do was call up Ben and make sure he'd gotten home okay. My grandmother must have suspected this, because she took the phone off the hook.

"Let it ring busy," she said. "Let him wonder."

"What if Mom calls? Or Dad?"

"She has a ten-kilometer run tomorrow in the desert. I wouldn't hold my breath," she said, pulling a cigarette out of her purse. "I was always afraid she'd snap. The tightly wound ones often do." She lit the cigarette and inhaled so deeply that her cheeks caved in.

"We're not going over forty miles per hour and we're not at the zoo," I said.

"Yeah, I tell people that so they think I'm quirky instead of an addict. Truth is, I snap if I go more than three hours without one. Damn tobacco companies. If I knew then what I know now, I never would have started. And I'd have learned Spanish. Whole damn planet is speaking it."

"Aye, Caramba," I said.

"You think like a winner, Tess Whistle," she said. "Now tell me about this Ben."

Chapter 13

Most teenage girls probably wouldn't enjoy having their sixty-eight-year-old maternal grandmother forced onto them as their sole caretaker. In my case, it was sort of an improvement. She took me out to fancy restaurants, helped me track down fashionable size-ten shoes, and she bought me a car. Yes, on Sunday, two days after her arrival, Ada Bernice Cappy purchased a used cherry red Honda Civic for me.

When the taxi dropped us off at Lloyd's No Bull Car Lot, I was sure that she was purchasing the car for herself. But then she said, "If we buy you a red car, you've got to watch out for the bacon."

"What?" I asked.

"You can't speed. The police are always looking for red speeding cars."

"I don't drive," I said.

"I thought this hick state handed out licenses at fifteen."

"They do," I said. "I mean, I've taken driver's ed. I have a permit."

"That's enough," she said. "I'll teach you the rest."

And because my grandmother showed up on the lot via a taxi, she had little room to negotiate. Clearly, she needed a vehicle.

"It's not the deal of the century," she said, handing me the keys.

At first, I didn't think I'd be able to drive. I know I'd done it before in driver's ed, but this was different. Suddenly, there weren't any limits. There wasn't some nervous guy who smelled like beef jerky sitting beside me with his own set of brakes. If I made a mistake, I could cause an accident. I adjusted the rearview mirror several times. And both of my side mirrors. And, before I started the vehicle, while the emergency brake was still engaged, I asked my grandma to stand behind the trunk and circle around the car toward me so that I could determine exactly where my blind spot was situated.

"Can you see me now?" she hollered after every inch she moved.

"Stop asking me that," I said. "The sound of your voice is throwing me off."

After I knew for certain where my blind spot

was located, and how big it was, my grandmother climbed back inside the car and I started it up.

"You act like you'd prefer a horse and buggy," she said.

"A car can become a lethal weapon."

"Same thing could be said about a shoelace. Or a dove."

"How could a dove become a lethal weapon?"

"Well, if it was somehow frozen and dropped from a high place, like the Empire State Building, the dove would most likely kill any soul unfortunate enough to be in its path. Imagine it: Why, the beak alone could crack a skull. They're strong, but not impervious."

I really wished she hadn't said that. The Empire State Building was on my list of destinations to check out when I ventured to New York to visit Zena. Now, I'd constantly be craning my neck toward the sky, worried about falling doves and other debris. I mean, if Zena ever made it to New York.

My grandmother turned out to be an excellent driving instructor. She didn't say much and never hounded me. Once, I hit a mailbox and all she said was, "I'd leave a note." Another time, when I creamed a skunk, she said, "Too much stink in this world, anyway."

When Monday rolled around, for the first time

ever, I got to drive to school. For some unknown reason, driving around with my grandma all weekend had really diminished my vehicular-related anxieties. I was excited to drive to school. I felt like I, too, had won the lottery. Except I was Zena-less. She hadn't called yet. Or written me a second letter. Ben said that I'd hear from her soon. My grandma said that I should stop obsessing about it.

It goes without saying that my feelings for Ben were growing stronger. I think the sudden departure of both Zena and my parents helped fuel this. Suddenly, he'd become more important than people I'd known my whole life. In English, listening to Mrs. Hovel dissect Sophocles, sitting behind Ben, watching his neck, I had my first official daydream about nearly having sex. Even though it was a tight squeeze, Ben and I almost made love in the backseat of my Civic. He told me over and over again that he loved me, that he wanted to marry me. I told him I loved him too, and that I couldn't wait to be his wife. When the bell rang and class was over, I felt very hot. I also felt like I hadn't learned anything, especially when it came to Sophocles.

"Are you okay?" Ben asked.

"I got a car," I said.

"I know. You told me about it on the phone and I came over and saw it."

Ben rubbed my shoulder, and my body felt electric and alive.

"Do you want to grab a burrito for lunch?" he asked.

"I thought I was your burrito," I said.

He laughed. "No, you're a taco and enchilada combination plate."

"A burrito sounds good."

Ben smiled at me. Then he walked off.

When I opened up my locker and saw all Zena's stuff in there, it hit me again that she was really gone. Without her, I would no longer be part of a safe duo. Together, we'd been like a couple of superheroes, traveling through high school unaffected by the social strata of cliques and clubs. We existed in our own college-bound world, one that was unfazed by sports, proms, hazing, assemblies, and cheerleaders. Now, I was an *uno*. And I didn't want to be an *uno*. *Unos* were vulnerable. And apt to be tripped by status-seeking underclassmen. Or squirted with a water gun in your crotch area or boob region. For an *uno*, such occurrences were pretty much routine happenings.

I walked to class contemplating my fate. Ben Easter was the obvious solution. If I firmly attached myself to him, I would be part of a safe duo again. Kind of like plankton growing on whales. Maybe that's not the best example.

"I can't wait for that burrito," I yelled after him. He'd made it all the way across the commons and he didn't turn back around. Maybe he didn't hear me.

Math droned on and on and on. The guy who came up with the idea of mixing numbers and letters to solve imaginary problems had way too much time on his hands. (Yes, I'm sure it was a guy.)

Ben and I drove to Taco Time to get our burritos. As we ate in his car, I kept trying to touch his hand.

"Tess, I'm eating," he said.

"I'm lonely," I said.

"But I'm right here."

He stared at me, very sympathetically, and sighed.

"Don't come unglued," he said. "I know you're going through a tough time. Why don't I take you for a drive tonight? We can watch the moon."

"I love the moon," I lied. Even before we'd talked it to death in English during our discussion of *Frankenstein*, I'd always found it to be unsettling—hanging there, affecting the moods of wild animals and influencing the tides.

All day long I thought about being alone with Ben. I had my second and third daydreams about almost having sex. Then I realized that there was an enormous problem. In my daydreams I was wearing an extremely attractive and lacy pair of panties and matching bra. But in real life, I hadn't bought a decent new bra or pair of panties. I needed to go to the mall—immediately.

But I didn't hotfoot it over there after school. My grandma may have been cool enough to buy me a car, but she wasn't a total pushover. She had demanded that I come home immediately after school. Partly, this was so I could drive her to Kline's for a bagel and a cappuccino. Partly, this was because at heart she was an extremely responsible human being.

Once she was seated with her bagel and cappuccino, I told her that I needed to go to the mall.

"What do you need at the mall?" my grandma asked. (She had been kind enough not to point out that while attempting to park, I'd bumped into the curb three times.)

"Stuff," I said. I think I blushed. Because my face felt warm and I looked down at the salt and pepper shakers.

"Do you need foundation?" she asked.

"I don't wear makeup. And if I did, I'd buy it at the drugstore. It's cheaper," I said, still looking at the salt and pepper shakers.

"Foundation is another word for practical lingerie. Have your breasts grown? Do you need a new brassiere? Do you need help measuring your bosom?"

My grandmother stared right at my chest as she asked her questions.

"That's very invasive of you," I whispered, folding my arms and covering them up. "And we're in public."

"Filling out is a thing to be proud of. Have you tried a push-up brassiere? I think it's good to hoist the girls up as high as possible."

My blushing intensified. My grandma noticed.

"Ah to be young," she said. "And embarrassed by your own breasts."

"I'm not embarrassed by them," I whispered. "I just don't talk about them at the bagel shop. They're sacred."

My grandmother shrugged. "Boobs are boobs. And yours are quite nice."

As I sat there, I couldn't wait to get to a phone and tell Ben about all my suffering. I'd been abandoned by my parents. My best friend had been shipped away. And my primary caregiver was obsessed with my breasts.

Actually, she turned out to be an asset. She knew exactly what I needed. After Kline's, she helped me buy the Supra Bra. She recommended that I buy it in light pink so I could wear it underneath whites. She also informed me that I could wear a 36B or a 34C. But when I chose the 34C, the fabric puckered over my right breast.

"No two boobs are alike," my grandmother said.

"I feel like a freak," I said. This was the first time I'd realized that my breasts were two different sizes.

"Only silicone racks look perfect. And even those come with their own set of problems," she said. "Yours look great."

I was surprised that my grandma was aware of breast implants and had used the word "rack." I was also surprised that she insisted that I buy several pairs of thongs to reduce unsightly panty lines. I was further surprised when she lit up a cigarette at the register and got us kicked out of Macy's.

"I'm a smoker, not a Communist," she said, huffing and puffing her way to the automatic doors.

I held my purchases close to me. I couldn't wait to show Ben.

Chapter 14

With my shoes on and lip gloss in place, I was all ready to stand in my doorjamb and wait for Ben. But then my grandmother pointed out that when I pressed myself between the front door and the screen, my face rubbed up against the screen's mesh.

"It turns your nose tip an ashy gray color," she said in a very serious tone.

I was surprised that Zena had never mentioned that to me.

"Maybe she thought it was just a birthmark," my grandma offered. "Unless they're shaped like historical figures, it's not polite to comment on people's birthmarks. Why don't you just wait inside the house?" She was resting on the couch, her dry-heeled, bare feet propped up on a pillow.

"I'm too polite," I said. Which I felt was the truth.

I'd always waited in plain view for Zena, so I'd never inconvenience her with a delay.

"Well, it looks a little desperate to me. Why don't you go out onto the road and just start walking toward him? If you leave now and are brisk about it, you could probably save him a quarter of a mile."

I frowned and walked out to the driveway.

Standing beneath the moonlit sky, I heard a dog bark, a coyote howl, and a cat unleash a sound that seemed to indicate that she was in heat. The noises made my skin goose pimple. I mean, even a domestic cat could have rabies. So I walked back inside the house. My grandmother, still on the couch, was completely engrossed in the official biography of Sacagawea and didn't even lift her eyes to look at me. But she nodded her approval.

"Did you know that Meriwether Lewis committed suicide?" she asked. "Being an explorer must be damn tough."

"Must be," I said.

When Ben rolled into the driveway, his headlights lit up the front window.

"Let him come to the door," my grandma said, licking her thumb and turning a page.

I did.

He knocked. I opened it. We left.

"You look great," Ben said, kissing my cheek.

I wrapped my arm around his waist and slipped my hand in his back pocket. He purred like a cat and kissed my cheek again.

"I thought we'd go for a ride," he said. He opened up my door and kissed the top of my head as I settled into his passenger's seat.

We drove to the top of Iona Hill and parked overlooking Idaho Falls. Countless house lights twinkled below us.

"What do you think they're all doing?" I asked.

"Probably watching the news," he said. "Cautious Bob's got a segment tonight about how to survive an avalanche."

"I feel like I don't even have to watch Cautious Bob to know what he'll say."

"What do you think his first tip will be?" Ben asked.

"Avoid climates that experience snow."

Ben laughed.

"Actually, you're supposed to form a fist and raise it above your head. It helps create a larger air pocket. Suffocation is what kills most avalanche victims."

"How do you know that?" Ben asked.

"Around this time last year, Cautious Bob did that same segment. It's a repeat."

Ben laughed harder.

"It's amazing that guy has a job," he said.

"It's probably because he's cute," I said.

Ben stopped laughing.

"You think Cautious Bob is cute? He's like thirty years old. And his hair's thinning. He'll be bald before he's forty."

"I didn't say I'd date him. I just said he was cute. I think certain varieties of trees are cute too. Like dogwoods."

Ben nodded. It didn't take long before we were kissing. Ben reclined his seat back, and I moved over on top of him. But when I heard a coyote howl, I bolted upright, smacking my head on the low roof. I checked to see if our doors were locked.

"What are you doing?" he asked.

"Did you hear that coyote? And your door wasn't even locked." His lock looked like a silver golf tee, and I pressed it down until it clicked.

"That was a dog, not a coyote. And unless it's Lassie, I doubt it'd be smart enough to open up a car door."

"You never know," I said, pulling on his door handle, double-checking that it was actually locked.

"Tess Whistle, what are you afraid of?" Ben reached up and unlocked his door.

"Don't do that!" I said, relocking it.

"Seriously, what are you afraid of?" He reached up again, but this time he didn't unlock the door. I think he saw the tears rolling down my cheeks.

"Tess," he said, pulling me to him, giving me a hug. "I'm sorry. I didn't mean to upset you. I didn't realize that you had a dog phobia. Were you bitten as a child?"

I twisted out of the embrace and rolled back into my own seat, sniffling. "I don't have a dog phobia," I said. "I have a wildlife phobia. I'm afraid of being eaten by wild animals."

"Wild dogs?" he asked.

"Not really wild dogs as much as wild animals like cougars or bears or wolves. But honestly, all animals frighten me." I wiped my tears away and turned to look at him. "Anyway, a lot of people get attacked by dogs. For mail carriers, it's a growing problem. And it's not like I'm crazy. A bunch of animals that you'd think wouldn't hurt a fly are intact with razor-sharp teeth and carry deadly diseases. For instance, there are racoons, and possums, and ticks."

After I said this, I realized that I wasn't sure if a tick actually was considered an animal. Also, I wasn't sure if those things had teeth.

Ben ran his fingers through my hair and held on to the back of my neck.

"But we're in a parked car," he said.

"I know," I whined.

"Do you want to know what I think?" he asked.

"I don't know. Are you going to make fun of me?"

"No. I think that we all carry around a certain amount of anxiety. We all worry about different things. For you, I think that wild animals are just a symbol for what you can't control in life. Deep down, I don't think you fear wolves and bears as much as you fear the unknown. It's just your way of dealing with the fact that the world isn't safe."

I didn't say anything. I just looked at him.

"Is it okay that I said that?" he asked. He let go of my neck and picked up my hand. He kissed it four times.

"But I don't know if I can change," I said. "I don't see myself becoming some sort of wolf or bear lover. I mean, if I saw a wounded wolf or something on the side of the road, I'd call someone to help it as soon as I got home, but I'd never put it in my car."

Ben laughed and kissed my hand again.

"I wouldn't want you to go around tossing wounded wolves in your trunk," he said.

"No," I interrupted. "I meant my backseat. I'd never stuff an animal in my trunk. I don't even think that's legal. Or humane. Plus, there's important wires back there an animal could gnaw through— your blinkers, and rear brake lights, and then there's your spare tire, and emergency flares—"

"Okay, I get it," he said. Ben looked like he wanted

to laugh again, but he didn't. "Tess, I don't think you have to change," he said. "Just be aware of it."

Ben leaned in and kissed me. Soon, we were fogging up the glass. It was easy to put the conversation out of my mind. My urge to get close took over, and I didn't have to think. About my parents. About Zena. About animals. About avalanches. All I had to do was feel. As I kissed Ben's neck, I moved my lips lower and lower, unbuttoning his shirt so I could continue to make southward progress.

"Tess," he said. "We should stop."

"What?" I asked. "Why?"

"Let's just sit and keep talking," he said.

"We can do that at school," I said, trying to kiss him again.

Ben pushed me away.

"What's wrong?" I asked.

"Nothing's wrong," he said.

I settled back into the passenger seat. My instincts told me that I should go along with what he was saying, to act like I was in agreement with this bad idea. But I couldn't.

"What's wrong?" I asked again.

"Nothing's wrong," he said. "It's just that you're going through a lot of changes. You're feeling vulnerable. I think we should stop."

"Is this because I was afraid of that dog?" I asked.

"No." He turned the key and started the engine.

I couldn't believe he was getting so philosophical on me. It's like he was suddenly my therapist or something.

"But you're a boy!"

"I don't want to take advantage of you."

"You're not," I said. "I like the way it feels." I tried to pull him to me, but he wouldn't come. "I agree with what you said. I am afraid of the unknown. But I'm not afraid of this. I want this." The windows and rearview mirror were caked with a thin coat of steam. Using his sleeve, Ben started wiping away a clear spot.

"I think I should take you home."

We'd been so busy talking about my fear of wildlife that I hadn't even had the chance to show Ben my Supra Bra.

"What did I do wrong?" I asked, tears rolling down my cheeks.

I'd never been the kind of girl who was quick to cry, but lately all of my emotions seemed to be right at the surface.

"This is too fast," he said.

"But you're a boy!" I yelled.

"What's that supposed to mean?"

"You're supposed to want it more than I do."

He put the car in reverse.

"Who says?"

"Don't play dumb. Everyone knows that boys are hornier. Your hormones are exploding. Boys your age who live in Wyoming are so out of control, they're having sex with sheep."

Ben pulled onto the road and drove the car down the hill.

"When it comes to sex, Tess Whistle, you've got bizarre ideas."

"Of course I do. We don't get cable!"

Ben laughed.

"I'm stopping because I like you," he said.

At this point, I didn't want to have sex. I wouldn't have had sex. I wasn't ready. But I didn't like the way this rejection felt. I wanted Ben to want me. I wanted to be the one who said when to stop.

"I just wanted to fool around," I said.

Ben squeezed my knee.

"We should slow down. Don't worry, we've got time."

I felt like Ben had thrown me a curveball.

I kept crying.

"Tess Whistle, I like you. A lot."

I didn't say anything.

"Let's play *Password*. The clue is 'immunizations.'"

I knew the answer he was fishing for was "Guatemala," but I didn't give it to him. Before I knew it, we were in my driveway. Ben turned off the car.

"I'll repeat the clue. 'Immunizations.'"

I think he was going to walk me to the front door, but I didn't give him the chance. I turned to him and yelled, "Guatemala!" Then, I ran to the house and didn't look back. When I flew inside, my grandmother was waiting on the couch, the book about Sacagawea fallen open over her chest. But I didn't stop to talk to her. I ran to my room and curled up on my bed.

Ben's rejection stung. It made me feel lonely. It reminded me of all the people I was losing in my life. The pain was centered in my chest. There was this tight, dark space inside of me that felt hurt and empty. Only three minutes had passed since I'd left the car, and I was already missing Ben. Or maybe I was really missing Zena.

I wished that I could have called and talked to her. She probably would have been disappointed in me. She's not a fan of blubbering. She would have told me I was a basket case and demanded that I snap out of it. "Why didn't he want me?" I'd ask her. "Why didn't he want to be close?" I can hear her huffing at me in exasperation. She'd point out that my feelings weren't all Ben's fault. Zena is brilliant. Even though it would have hurt, she would have told me that the bigger problem was myself.

Chapter 15

It took two more days before i had the opportunity to show Ben my new Supra Bra. For some reason, he'd become obsessed with getting into college. So when he wasn't with me, he was studying all the time.

"Come over," I pleaded. I was sitting on my bed, surrounded by my newly acquired thongs.

"I need to read *Macbeth*," he said.

"Mrs. Hovel didn't assign that," I said.

"I know. But by the time you get to college, most kids have read some Shakespeare. It's absolutely bizarre that this school district doesn't assign him."

"He slept around," I said.

"He's still a literary icon."

The fact that Ben was so concerned about getting a scholarship to UC San Diego and Scripps Institution of Oceanography, an out-of-state college, should have raised an enormous red flag. But it didn't. All I was concerned with was showing him my Supra Bra.

"Read one more chapter and then come over," I said.

"It's a play. It's told in acts," he said.

"My grandmother is driving me nuts. She wants to go bowling and then grab a martini."

"What's so bad about that?" he asked.

"She screams when she bowls. At the ball. At the pins. At the people in the other lanes. And she likes to get her martini at the Stardust, and that place really isn't suitable for teenagers. They have a very inappropriate comedian."

"They let you in?"

"It's a restaurant. The comedian performs in the bar area, but he's so loud that you can hear his act. He complains about women. Their big butts. Their mood swings and menstrual cramps. It annoys me. Rescue me," I said.

"Tess," he said. "I can't."

"You can," I said. "You just don't want to."

With that, I hung up the phone and marched downstairs and complained to my grandmother that I did not want to go bowling or to the Stardust.

"What should we do?" she grunted. My grandmother was crouched in the corner of the living room. She was in the middle of hefting my mother's favorite ficus tree into a new terra-cotta pot.

"It's a school night. I should probably study," I said.

"Sounds reasonable," she replied. "Were you talking on the phone to Ben? Did you two get in a fight? Is that why your panties are in a bunch?" She scooped soil from the ficus tree's former pot and patted it around the replanted tree's base.

"We weren't fighting. We were having a disagreement," I said.

"When it comes to dating, there are rules." She stood up and pointed her finger at me with such passion that a small clump of potting soil sailed across the room and pelted me in the chest. "First, no man likes a nag. Remember that." She nodded her head with such enthusiasm that her blond hair continued to bounce even after her head had stopped moving. "Second, you need to let him chase you. Sure, you can let him catch you, but you should always be moving away.

"When I was eight, my neighbor bought a white-throated capuchin monkey named Bismarck. Every time I leaned in to kiss Bismarck, he would pull away. When I puckered up and dove in fast, he pulled back just as fast. When I cautiously snuck up on him, he slowly inched away. Men are a lot like capuchin monkeys. They don't like to be crowded, especially by lips. And remember this, Tess. Bismarck's refusal to kiss me made me want to kiss him all the more."

"Ben is not a monkey," I said. "Besides, he loves it when I call him."

My grandmother raised her eyebrows. Then she leaned close to me and tried to kiss me.

"Grandma," I said pulling away.

"Next time you're at a cemetery, look around at all the headstones. They're side by side. Even married couples. Nobody wants a plot on top of another person's plot. Why?" She clapped her bare hands over the new terra-cotta pot, casting away some loose dirt. "Even when they're dead, people still love their own space."

When I heard a knock at the door, I didn't even have time to hope that it was Ben. But it was. He looked frustrated. My grandmother wiped her hands on her pants and let him in. Then she said, "Tess, I think I'm going to get my sneakers and go for a run."

"Okay," I said.

"I'm going to move really fast and run away from the house," she said. "I'm not going to let anything touch me. Call me Bismarck."

Ben wrinkled his face in confusion and plopped down on the sofa. My grandma slipped on her coat and shoes and bolted out the door, squealing like a monkey as she went. I collapsed next to Ben and said, "Don't ask."

I tried to cuddle up next to him, but he was as stiff as an unaffectionate board.

"Don't," he said. "I came to talk."

"Okay," I said. "Did you finish *Macbeth*?"

"No, Tess. You hung up on me and so I drove over here."

"I'm sorry about that," I said, kissing his neck. "But I wanted to show you something." I began to unbutton my blouse.

"Tess, that's not why I'm here. We need to talk."

And, suddenly, I realized that Ben *was* like a capuchin monkey. I was so lucky that my grandmother had clued me in on this before she left. Because I realized exactly what I needed to say.

I stood up from the couch and held my hand up in the air like I was stopping traffic.

"Ben, you can't come barging in on me anytime you like. I do need *some* space."

His mouth dropped open, and I could see all the way back to his cute, cavity-free molars.

"But you hung up on me and I came over to talk," he said.

"I hung up because I was through talking."

"Tess, ever since we started getting physical, you've been acting different."

Finally, I saw the light. If I were a cartoon
character, an enormous lightbulb floating above
my head would have popped on. "Maybe we should
stop getting physical," I said. It killed me to say this,
because what I wanted most, regardless of whether
or not it was normal, was to rip his shirt off and
tongue-bathe every inch of his chest. "You're right,
I've been placing way too much emphasis on it."

"I'm not saying we should stop. We just need
balance."

"Exactly," I said. "You should go home. We should
take the week off." My insides were convulsing. I'd
started to sweat. I needed Ben like I needed air. I
prayed he'd object to this. And he did.

"I don't think we need to do anything drastic," he
said. "I really like you."

He reached for my hand, and I pulled away. I
stood up and started pacing. "I don't know," I said.
Ben came over and joined me. Then, I acted like I
was a capuchin monkey and I pulled away from his
face as he leaned in to kiss me. Apparently, there can
only be one capuchin monkey in a relationship. Ben
kept trying to get closer. I kept pulling away.

Finally, I let him kiss me. It was a deep and
frustrated kiss. It started on my mouth and went to
my neck, and then he asked, "What did you want to
show me?"

"I got a Supra Bra," I said, nibbling on his earlobe.

Ben and I walked upstairs to my bedroom. He lifted up my shirt and looked at my soft pink bra.

"It's nice," he said.

He kissed my breasts through the bra and I thought I was going to melt away like I was made of wax.

"Is this okay?" he asked.

"Mmmm, Guatemala," I said.

By the way he was breathing, I could tell he was holding back laughter. I ran my fingers through his curly hair and pushed his head away from my chest. I wanted him to stay close, but this new monkey business was paying off.

"I'm done," I said.

"You are?" he asked.

Then the front door slammed.

"Do you two want brownies? I've been craving them all week. Something about having a pan hanging on the wall, I guess. I like to eat them half-baked and resembling batter, but if you want me to bake them all the way, I will." Then she squealed again, like a monkey.

"Your grandma sounds like Tarzan's chimp, Cheeta."

"That's not polite."

"Is it a good idea for you to eat brownies?" he asked.

I quickly realized he was talking about my sugar issues and not my weight, so I didn't get offended.

"It's okay if I just eat a sliver," I said.

Ben nodded, but still looked a bit concerned.

"I'll take mine fully baked," I hollered. (Anything containing eggs should be thoroughly cooked.)

"Ditto," Ben yelled.

"Suit yourselves," she called.

I slipped my shirt back on, and Ben took my hand and led me down the stairs.

Chapter 16

The problem with acting like a capuchin monkey when deep down you're nothing like a capuchin monkey is that you can't be true to yourself. Abandoning my true self made me a little uncomfortable. I had to keep telling myself that I was doing it for love. Plus, the capuchin monkey strategy was totally working. And it wasn't like I was hurting anybody. So I figured that it was okay.

Around the third week of December, my parents decided to resurface for the holidays. They didn't come home. They called and asked me and my grandmother to visit them in Utah. At first, I wasn't thrilled about leaving Ben. But my grandmother assured me that absence makes the heart grow fonder.

"For instance," she said, "take Elvis Presley. After he died, he became more popular than buttered popcorn. Same thing happened with Barry Manilow."

"Barry Manilow is still alive," I said, folding a pair of jeans and putting them in my suitcase.

"Good to know," she said. My grandmother carried her packed suitcase to the threshold of my door. She'd ordered it out of a funky catalog the weekend after she arrived. I guess she anticipated that she'd be traveling. It was bright green and plastered with pink butterflies. And for some unknown reason, she'd tied a wad of orange yarn to the handle.

"What's this for?" I asked, fingering the yarn.

"So I can distinguish it from other bags," she said.

I let that statement pass without comment.

"I'll load everything in the morning," I said. "I'm ready for bed."

"Suit yourself. Sleep like a rock. I know I will."

Ben called right as I was drifting off.

GRANDMA: "Tess, telephone."

ME: "I thought you were sleeping like a rock."

GRANDMA: "Apparently, I respond to ringing."

ME: "Hello?"

BEN: "It's me."

ME: "Hi, Bob. I really enjoyed your segment on avalanches tonight. Especially that part about wearing a beacon. You look so dreamy in snow pants. I can tell you lift weights. What did I ever do to deserve you?"

BEN: "Very funny. I'm calling to wish you a safe drive."

ME: "That's very thoughtful of you."

BEN: "I was also wondering what you want to do about presents?"

ME: "That's very self-centered of you."

BEN: "I'm being serious. How about we exchange gifts when you get back on the twenty-eighth?"

ME: "That works. Don't miss me too much while I'm gone."

BEN: "I'll only miss you every other day."

ME: "Is tomorrow a day off or day on?"

BEN: "Day on."

ME: "Then I'll miss you right back."

We didn't talk too long. And I was glad that we weren't exchanging gifts until the twenty-eighth. I hadn't bought his yet. I was hoping to find something in Utah. Like maybe a uniquely carved rock or something.

About four minutes after I hung up with Ben, Zena called me for the first time since she'd been shipped away. When the phone rang, I picked it up on the first ring because I thought it was Ben calling me back to say something supersweet. It wasn't. Unfortunately, it was a sad conversation.

ZENA: "I wish I'd never built that stinking bomb. Everybody thinks I'm crazy."

ME: "Zena? Is that you?"

ZENA: "Do you have another bomb-building friend?"

ME: "How are you? What's going on?"

ZENA: "I'm miserable. I hate Arizona. The heat is debilitating. My body is ready to experience winter. My mother came to visit dressed like a hooker—lots of red lipstick—and my father is still mad at me. They're getting divorced. I think he's going to marry Mindy."

ME: "Don't cry. Things will get better."

ZENA: "I'm calling to let you know that while I'm here, you can drive my car."

ME: "That's so sweet of you, but my grandmother bought me a car."

ZENA: (Sobbing) "What? Are you kidding? That's just like you. Everything works out for Tess Whistle. I bet you end up winning the lottery, too. I hate people like you. I hope you never come to visit. I hope I never see you again." (Sobbing)

ME: "Zena? Zena?"

When it came to playing the part of a capuchin monkey, Zena was a master of the craft. She pulled away from me so hard that it was impossible for me to make her come close again. After she hung up on me, I couldn't help myself from calling Ben. He seemed very sympathetic at first. But then he wanted to talk about college and the future.

"But this is eating me alive!" I said.

"Maybe you should write her a letter," he suggested.

And so I wrapped things up with Ben, pulled myself out of bed, and then sat down and wrote Zena a long letter.

I told her that I loved her. And I told her about my messy life and how I feared that my father had been fired from his job at the hospital because he hadn't shown up to work in weeks. I told her that I'd recently discovered that my breasts weren't the same size, and I asked her if her breasts were like that too. I also told her about how much I loved Ben and I asked her if she'd heard from Robert. I told her that I didn't worry about getting a ring anymore, because I'd come to realize that love wasn't about that. I begged her to write me back. And I thanked her for the offer to drive her car. I told her I understood why she built the bomb. I told her that I probably would have done the same thing. (I didn't know if that was exactly true, but I thought it would make her feel better.)

I told her I was off to visit my parents in Utah. Then I asked her what the odds were that all four of our parents would have meltdowns at the exact same time? Then I crossed out the word "meltdown" and wrote "freaky problems" because, technically speaking, I think Zena had had a "meltdown" and I didn't want her to think I was judging her.

Then I opened my wallet, pulled out the fifty my father had given me, and slipped it in the envelope. In sixth grade, Zena had been a hardcore Twizzler addict. She even carried a few spare sticks wrapped in plastic Baggies in her shoes. At the bottom of my note I scribbled: "In hopes that you'll buy some Twizzlers, remember me fondly, and have a Merry Christmas." I put a snowman stamp on the envelope and dropped it in the mailbox. Then, I slept like a rock.

My grandmother and I left early the next morning, before the sun was even up. Loading our suitcases into the trunk, my stomach felt like it was eating itself. I was half asleep and a nervous wreck and I had no idea why. I'd written to Zena. Things were stable with Ben. And my grandma would probably sleep and not hassle me while I drove.

I slammed the trunk and got behind the wheel. Suddenly, it was as though my grandmother and I were seated inside of a freshly shaken snow globe. Small white flakes dropped onto the windshield and drifted down the glass. I turned on the wipers. This was the first long distance I had ever driven, and I was going to have to do it in snow. Maybe we should reschedule our trip. It wasn't like I had an irrational fear of snow. Although, I'd never been fond of the Swiss Alps, ski poles, or malamutes. My grandma used her sixth sense and figured out that I was worried.

"I put studded tires on the car," she said. "As long as you don't drive like a teenager, we'll be fine."

"But I am a teenager," I said.

"Drive like you're forty."

I backed out of the driveway and headed to town. I drove through downtown Idaho Falls and merged onto the freeway. My grandma was very respectful and didn't try to distract me with conversation. Instead, she sucked on hard candy, which created a slightly annoying slurping sound, but it was something I could deal with. Soon, the silence grew unbearable, and an hour later, as snow continued to lightly fall and we zoomed past Pocatello, my grandma unleashed a torrent of questions.

"Sexually speaking, how far have you and Ben gone?"

"Grandma!" I yelled, keeping my eyes locked on the road. "I'm still a virgin."

"I can appreciate that. In fact, I think that's a good thing."

We drove another mile. Then she said, "I was a virgin when I married your grandfather, but I'm not sure if I'd do it that way again. I never sampled another man. And the wedding night hurt like hell. I think if I could do it over again, I might have slept with more men. Especially after your grandpa passed away. God rest his soul."

"Grandma! You shouldn't say things like that."

"I'm just talking."

"Let's talk about something else."

"Of course, I would have used protection. You do plan on using protection, right?" she asked.

"I'm not talking about this."

"Don't be that way." She reached into her purse and pulled out a cigarette. "The wind will suck most of this smoke right out the window. You won't even notice."

I started to cough anyway.

"Cut your grandma some slack."

She smoked, and the conversation died out. Thank God! But an hour later, by the time we reached Malad Pass, she was ready to talk again.

"It's awful about Ben's cancer," she said.

"How did you know about that?"

"Once, last week, you went to the bathroom and were gone a real long time and we struck up a conversation and it just came out. By the way, you probably need more fiber in your diet."

"My fiber is fine! And he doesn't like to talk about his cancer," I said.

"He did with me."

"What did he say?"

"We talked about his diagnosis. And how during his chemotherapy treatments he was looking through the cupboard for a granola bar and came across a jar of spaghetti sauce and read the expiration date and wondered if the sauce was going to outlive him."

"He did not!" I said.

"He did so."

"Well, maybe he does want to talk about it. But it's so sad, Grandma. In the pictures I saw, he looked so sick."

"Life isn't a party where all they serve is punch and pie. There's tough stuff, too," she said.

"His cancer is too tough for me."

"I imagine it's tough for him, too."

"But health issues are so big and serious, and our relationship is more about relaxing and having fun."

She didn't say anything.

"What else have you two talked about?" I asked.

"Well, he asked how old you were when you were diagnosed with diabetes."

I could feel my grandmother's stare burning a hole in the side of my head.

"He did not! What did you say?"

"Relax. I didn't tell him the truth." She took her stare and positioned it out the windshield. "Tess, it's one thing to play hard to get and act like a capuchin monkey, but it's quite another thing to lie about a serious medical condition."

"It was a total accident!"

And when I said the word "accident," it was as if the car somehow knew it was supposed to spin out of control. It happened so fast. I remember the back end of my Honda passing the front end. And I remember watching the landscape swirl around me. And I remember, quite vividly, that before the impact happened, as the car was racing over the fog line, that I saw an enormous horse standing in the median. Then I heard my grandmother yell, "Moose!" And then I heard a horrific noise. And the world went black.

Apparently, I hit a patch of black ice. I was told this by the doctor after I woke up in the hospital, my head aching, my right arm slung across my chest in a plaster cast. My grandmother supplied more details. She said that when the car went out of control, I cursed like a sailor, that I hit the brakes and skidded into the median, then into the moose. She said that my head struck the steering wheel, that the tail end of the car is what collided with the moose. She said it was that impact that popped open our trunk and sent all of our suitcases tumbling out. She said that when the suitcases hit the asphalt they exploded and that all the rubberneckers saw everything from our underwear to our toothbrushes scattered along the road in the snow.

She pointed out that it was a fortunate thing that we'd bought me new underwear. Then she said that the paramedics hauled me onto a gurney and wheeled me passed the deceased moose to get me to the ambulance. She said that before the doors shut and she was hauled away in a separate ambulance that she heard me scream, "I'm not a diabetic. I lied."

After my grandmother offered up all these incredible details, I closed my eyes and fell back asleep. In all my life, I'd never been so tired. In all my life, I'd never been forced to endure such a long, disastrous day.

Chapter 17

My parents drove up from Utah and when I woke up on the second day and saw them standing over me, I said the first thing that came to my mind.

"You look Hispanic!"

"They are quite tan," my grandmother said.

"How are you feeling? How are your ribs?" asked my father.

At that point, I realized that my rib area was sore.

"Did I break my ribs?" I asked.

"No, precious, you cracked them." My mother reached down and kissed my forehead. She looked young and different. And totally Latino.

"Are we part Puerto Rican?" I asked.

"Who knows? We're complete mutts," said my grandmother. "Maybe when you get better we can do our genealogy. I've always wanted to trace our lineage back to find out whether or not we're related to British kings."

My mother sighed. My father stood beside her and rubbed her back. Their faces looked very suspicious and apologetic. My grandmother refused to make eye contact with me and began to whistle.

"What's going on?" I asked.

"You've been in an accident," said my mother.

"I know that!" I said.

Everyone was silent. I could hear my IV drip and the steady hum of the muted television set that hung in the upper corner of my sanitary white room. Then, out of nowhere, I yelled, "I'm not moving to Utah."

I didn't know why I had said this or where this idea had come from. My parents looked at each other.

"Did you tell her?" asked my mother.

"No," said my father.

"I didn't say anything," said my grandmother, folding her arms across her chest. She looked perturbed. "You probably mentioned it while she was unconscious and she picked up on it. Just because somebody isn't conscious doesn't mean that they don't have their wits about them."

"I'll keep that in mind," said my father.

"You can finish out the school year," said my mother. "But your father has taken a job at a hospital in St. George. And Harrison has hired me on at a ropes course." She smiled at me and rubbed my hand.

"What about me!" I said. "I've got a broken arm."

"We're going to stay put until summer," said my grandma. "Your parents plan on visiting every other weekend. I think it's criminal and that they've completely abdicated their roles as parents. If she weren't my daughter, I'd sic child welfare on her. But I don't believe in turning in relatives, unless they've committed murder or kidnaped somebody or stolen art from a good museum—"

"Idaho was killing us," my mother interrupted. "All those cows. All those potatoes." As my mother spoke, she began to cry. "I'm not cut out to be an Idahoan. All that snow. All that wind. And we're so close to Montana."

"What's wrong with Montana?" I asked.

"Deranged people live in Montana. They don't even have a speed limit," said my mother. "The state is loaded with feral dogs. And now they've let wolves live there."

I knew that this was a bunch of bull. I mean, Yellowstone had continued to move in gray wolves, but I didn't think that was the true motivation behind my parents' decision to relocate. And Utah? California was a state I could have considered, but Utah?

My grandmother shook her head. "Just because you want to live in Utah doesn't give you the right to denigrate Montana," she said. "It's a lovely state. Big sky. Big rivers. Big goats."

My parents scowled at her. I closed my eyes. "Is Ben coming to visit?" I asked.

"Ben and his family sent you those," my grandmother said, pointing to a large arrangement of mixed flowers. "There's quite a storm outside, and you're getting released tomorrow, so I don't think he's driving up."

"Does Zena know?" I asked.

"No, dear. I called her aunt and she's decided to withhold the news of your accident. Apparently, some stripper Zena idolized lost her life under similar conditions. Zena's aunt was afraid it might alarm her."

"She wasn't a stripper," I said. "She was a poet who occasionally ate fire while topless."

"Well, where I come from, if a woman jiggles the girls onstage for Washingtons, even if she's wearing pasties, she's considered a stripper. I don't care if she has a second act."

My grandmother walked to my side and held my hand. It was clear from the blank looks on my parents' faces that they didn't know who Ben was. Or that Zena was living in the desert. And I didn't bother filling them in. If they wanted to run off to Harrison Q. Hart's survival camp in Utah and abandon me, their only child, they should feel a little left out of the loop.

Chapter 18

I woke up in the hospital and I didn't know what time it was. My grandmother sat beside me watching the TV up in the corner at a volume that was so soft, I was sure she was missing 90 percent of what was being said.

"Do you want water?" she asked. She walked to the sink and filled a paper cup. Her hands were shaking. "Your parents are in the cafeteria getting dinner. They'll be back soon." She looked at me and forced a smile.

I raised my head as she held the cup to my lips, tilting a cool flow of water into my mouth. When I was finished, I turned my head and a cold stream slipped down my neck.

"Oh, gosh," she said, mopping up the spill with my stiff hospital sheet.

"Thanks," I said.

"Tess, I want you to know that I realize that this was my fault and that I'm sorry and that I'm going to quit smoking. In fact, I already have."

I turned my head to face her, and the pillow made a crunching sound. Apparently, hospital laundry rooms use a considerable amount of starch.

"It's not your fault. You didn't put that moose there."

My grandmother sat down next to me and firmly held my hand.

"I put you in the driver's seat. It was a mistake. I realize that and I'm sorry. Your mother is right. I'm carefree to the point of being a danger to others. And winning the Illinois lottery hasn't improved this. My pie-in-the-sky attitude consistently leads me into making impulsive decisions. It's my poor decision-making skills that led us straight into that moose and got us into this disaster."

"I don't really think it's a disaster," I said. "We're going to be fine. And if Mom and Dad hadn't run off to Utah, we never would have been headed south on I-15 in a snowstorm in the first place. You have my permission—go ahead and blame them. And don't beat yourself up for winning the lottery. You should be happy. It means you're lucky."

My grandmother was taking the accident way too seriously. I mean, it was serious, but not so serious that it should have made her doubt her worthiness as a grandmother. She put her face in her hands and started to cry.

"Let's not blame anybody. Let's just blame the moose," I said.

"This is such a mess. You deserve better, Tess. I want to make it up to you. I plan to stay with you as long as you want."

Some teenagers might not have been thrilled to hear their sixty-eight-year-old maternal grandmother make such a pledge at their hospital bedside, but I found it reassuring.

My grandmother squeezed my hand again and patted it a few times. Then there was a soft knock at the door, and she used the corner of my stiff bed sheet to dab at her eyes. "This room needs some Kleenex."

I laughed. When she opened the door, both of us were totally surprised to see Benjamin Easter standing in the hallway.

"I know visiting hours are almost over. I was hoping I could say hello to Tess." Ben's hair looked wild; his curls were going everywhere, some were flat, some were balls of frizz. Even from across the room, I could tell that his eyes were bloodshot. My grandmother stepped aside.

"I think I'll go to the coffee machine and get something. Maybe coffee," she said.

Ben walked forward, and the door swung closed behind him. He stood over me, staring at me like I was a piece of rare art.

"Tess," he said. "You're alive."

Considering that I only had minor injuries, I thought that comment was a tad melodramatic. So I laughed.

"It takes more than a moose to stop me."

"Tess." He leaned in and cradled my face with his hands. "I thought you were dead."

"I didn't realize you were such a fatalist," I said. I didn't like the idea that Ben had heard about my accident and leaped to the conclusion that I'd been killed. It seemed entirely too pessimistic, especially for a cancer survivor.

"No, my parents told me you were in a car accident. As soon as they told me, I got in my car and started to drive to you. But the radio mentioned a crash on I-15 that had killed a woman. I thought it was you. I thought it was you," he said. I felt Ben's weight on top of me. He was hugging me hard and pressing himself against me.

"My arm," I said, pushing back a bit.

"I'm sorry," he said. "I'm so glad you're going to be okay."

"Me too," I said.

Ben leaned in again and kissed me. I kissed him back.

"I love you, Tess," he said. He stood over me smiling, brushing his hand against my face. "I love you and I want this relationship to work. No more slowing down."

I remember being shocked to hear somebody I wasn't related to profess their love for me. It felt good. Then it hit me. Ben's belief that I had been killed was the ultimate capuchin monkey move. He couldn't get close enough.

My grandmother walked back in holding a Styrofoam cup topped with an inch of whipped cream. "The picture of the hot chocolate looked better than the one of the coffee," she said. Then she picked up the remote control and turned up the volume on the TV. "You'll never guess what story they're running on CNN."

My grandma was right; the story was unbelievable. Earlier that day, in Terre Haute, Indiana, a family was awakened by a big crash. They ran to the source of the noise, their infant daughter's nursery. There, they found a large hole had been ripped open in their ceiling and their baby's changing table had been reduced to splinters.

At first, they thought their house had been hit by a meteorite. But it was later determined that it had been airplane waste. An enormous wad of frozen crap had almost killed this family's slumbering baby girl. The family was hugging and kissing and pointing to the destruction. "It's the happiest day of my life," the mother said, kissing her big-headed, bawling child.

"Can you believe that? I mean, can you believe that?" my grandma asked, turning the volume back down.

"That's bizarre stuff," said Ben, wiping away his tears.

"It is a very moving story," she said.

As much as I wanted to talk or think deeply and explore the uncanny significance of an event Zena had spoken about months ago actually happening, I was too exhausted.

"Is it okay if I sleep in the waiting room?" Ben asked.

"That's fine with me," I said, smiling.

"Let me get you a pillow," said my grandma, opening up a closet door near the TV.

If my parents came back in, I didn't hear them. I drifted off to sleep thinking about how happy I was to be dating such a great guy like Ben. And how lucky that family was in Indiana. I didn't know how many people falling airplane waste had ever killed, but I thought that any number was too high.

Chapter 19

The following afternoon, I was released. a nurse pushed me out of the hospital's automatic front doors in a squeaky wheelchair that relentlessly pulled to the left. She handed me a small sack of free random items ranging from mouthwash to a packet of shampoo that didn't require water. In big block letters on the front, the metallic pouch stated: PRODUCT DOES NOT PRODUCE A LATHER. It seemed utterly unnatural, like astronaut shampoo or something.

I was assigned to ride home in my father's goldenrod Buick Le Sabre. My mother would join us. Ben and my grandmother went in his car. I no longer had a car. The exact words my grandma used when describing it were: "That baby's a total loss."

On the drive home, my father let me ride in the

front passenger seat. My mother sat in the back and talked endlessly about all of the wilderness knowledge she'd gained at Hart Valley Ranch.

MY MOTHER: "In the last century, black bears and grizzly bears killed one hundred and thirty-three people in this country."

MY FATHER: "Actually, Rita, that statistic includes Canada."

MY MOTHER: "People need to wise up. Grizzlies aren't the only bear on the block that will kill you."

MY FATHER: "Bears are so misunderstood."

MY MOTHER: "Tess, did you know that you can't outrun a bear?"

ME: "Don't I just have to be able to run faster than the person I'm with?"

MY FATHER: "There's a lot of truth to that."

MY MOTHER: "Do you know the difference between a defensive or an aggressive attack? It could save your life."

ME: "High school doesn't really offer bear courses."

MY MOTHER: "It's almost like a conspiracy. Like somebody out there wants bear-related teen deaths to increase."

MY FATHER: "Rita, calm down."

MY MOTHER: "Tess, in a defensive encounter you're dealing with a stressed bear, usually a grizzly. It may charge. Keep in mind, most charges stop short. Stand your ground. Facing a defensive bear may be very difficult, and be prepared for its insufferable bad breath. It will be hard, but talk to the bear in a calm voice."

ME: "What makes a bear stressed?"

MY FATHER: "Usually when you enter its personal space."

MY MOTHER: "Tess, if a defensive bear attacks, fall to the ground. Lie on your stomach with your legs spread apart and lock your fingers behind your head. You need to protect your face and neck. A defensive bear enjoys focusing its attack on a person's face."

ME: "I'll try."

MY MOTHER: "Tess, I've seen pictures of survivors. Protect your face!"

MY FATHER: "And if the bear flips you over, roll until your stomach and vital organs are protected against the ground. Don't struggle with the bear. Play dead. And do not cry out."

ME: "Have you ever seen a bear in the wild?"

MY MOTHER: "Of course not, we wear bells."

MY FATHER: "Now, Tess, listen to your mother, an aggressive encounter will most likely put you face to snout with a black bear. And an aggressive encounter with a bear needs to be handled a lot differently than a defensive encounter."

ME: "Do I punch it or something?"

MY MOTHER: "Exactly! Well, not initially. First, remain calm and talk to the bear in a firm voice. Show it your hands so it can see you're not another bear. Then, assess your situation and try to move away from the bear. That may be all it wants."

ME: "Because I'm in its personal space."

MY MOTHER: "Exactly."

MY FATHER: "But you still need to watch the bear. If it follows you, you've probably got an aggressive bear, and this is a dangerous situation. The bear may have been curious or testing you. But if you don't stand your ground, it may turn predatory. If that happens . . ."

MY MOTHER: "Oh, God, let's hope that doesn't happen."

MY FATHER: "Tess, if that happens, you've got to act aggressively. Let that bear know that you'll fight it. The more the bear persists, the more aggressive you need to be. Yell at it. Stare that bear right in the eye and make yourself look as big as possible. Then, stamp your feet and take a step toward it. Also, if you've got bear spray, this is a good time to use it."

MY MOTHER: "Yes, and if it attacks, you fight, Tess. Kick and punch and hit that predatory bear. Focus on its eyes and nose."

ME: "You make it sound like boxing."

MY MOTHER: "If it helps to think of it that way, then yes, box the bear."

MY FATHER: "It's not true that bears merely maul people. They will eat your remains."

ME: "Thanks for the heads-up."

MY FATHER: "I'm so glad we took the time to have this talk. This is essential information."

MY MOTHER: "It is. So remember, in a defensive attack, play dead, and in a predatory attack, kick that bear's ass."

MY FATHER: "Rita, you swore."

MY MOTHER: "For punctuation."

I didn't say anything more. Instead, I sat and thought very hard about what Ben and I had talked about that night on Iona Hill, about why I feared wild animals. I still thought he was right. Because honestly, in all my life, I'd never once seen a bear in the wild. Even though I drove through Yellowstone Park with my family every year, puttering along mountain roads at ten miles per hour, I'd never even caught a glimpse of one of those furry beasts lumbering behind the trees. Elk? Yes. Buffalo? Certainly. Marmots? Of course. Bears? Never. So why had I lived so much of my life fairly certain that I would eventually be mauled to death? It had to be fear. Fear of what I couldn't control. Fear of the unknown.

I think that after striking a moose dead at sixty miles per hour, I began to understand how spending countless hours creating unlikely scenarios in which wild animals could ambush me and gnaw off my limbs was not the best use of my time. Listening to my parents fret about bear safety for two hours really drove this point home.

It felt good to walk inside my house. My parents were both extremely impressed with how clean my grandmother was keeping the place.

"Spic and span," my mother said, running her finger along a baseboard in the living room. "And she even repotted my ficus tree."

I smiled.

"We need to go to the grocery story," my father said, after taking a long hard look inside the refrigerator and cupboards. "We need to stock up for Christmas dinner."

"When is Christmas?" I asked.

"Tomorrow," my grandma said, bounding through the front door, chomping off the corner of a Rice Krispies Treat that was the size of a shoe box.

"You two shop and I'll stay with Tess," she said.

My parents exchanged a nervous glance.

"We've got to move forward," said my grandma. "You can't blame me forever."

My parents didn't answer her with words. They unloaded their luggage from the car, took it up to their room, then joined me on the couch and asked what I wanted from the grocery store. The two of them wrote up a thorough, two-page list.

"Wait," my grandma called. "Tess, do you need underpants?"

I shook my head no.

"She lost nearly her whole stash in the wreck. And nobody even bothered salvaging them. Not the firemen or the police. A lot of them still had the price tags on them."

My mother closed her eyes and licked her lips. "When there's an accident resulting in serious injuries, I think they let the underpants sit."

"I think the tow truck driver took them. I think tow truck drivers take a lot of things."

Nobody asked her to elaborate on this comment. But it made me smile. I was happy to see my grandmother's spunk returning. Self-loathing and moping just weren't in her nature. My grandmother helped me up to my room, and I crawled into my bed.

"How do you feel?" she asked.

"My ribs hurt. My arm is sore. I think I'd like some water," I said.

"I'll get you some water, but that's not what I mean." My grandmother picked up my hand and rubbed it. "This is an ordeal, Tess Whistle."

"Accidents happen," I said. The wreck seemed easy enough to get over, considering the silver lining that had emerged concerning my relationship with Ben.

"No. That's not what I mean. The last few months for you have been an ordeal. I'm worried about you. I want you to talk to me."

"Grandma," I said. "I'm fine. I'm just thirsty."

"This is a lot to experience," she said.

I raised my plaster cast and laughed. "I know, I've been fractured."

My grandmother stood up, exhaling a deep, frustrated breath. She walked to the doorway of my darkened room, clicked on the lamp on my dresser, and turned and looked at me. The way she was lit up from behind emphasized all of her wrinkles. She looked old.

"I'm good," I said.

"I'm glad. Until this accident I thought the second worst day of my life had been the day they announced the six winning lottery numbers. Your grandfather's stroke was, of course, the worst."

"Finding out you had the winning numbers should have been a fantastic day," I said.

My grandmother laughed and came and sat at the foot of my bed. "I thought I'd lost the ticket. I couldn't find it anywhere and I knew that I'd picked the winning numbers."

"I've never heard this."

"Well, I've never told anyone before. I felt so stupid. I couldn't believe I'd lost it. I tore the whole house apart looking for it; I even searched the garage and dug through the trash. I even dug through our neighbors' trash, which did nothing to improve my reputation in that community."

My grandmother took a deep breath and closed her eyes.

"The whole time it was in my apron pocket, the one your grandpa had given me for Mother's Day, the one that said 'Kiss the Cook.'"

"That's quite a story."

"It was such a long day. But not as long as yesterday."

"Grandma, how did you pick those numbers?"

"Ages," she said.

"Ages?"

"Yes, the age when Bismarck the capuchin monkey died, the age when I lost my virginity, the age when I had your mother, the age when I moved to Chicago, the age when you were born, and the age when your grandpa died. 11-19-22-35-52-13."

"You weren't thirteen when grandpa died."

"No, I was sixty-seven. I added the six and seven together. You can only choose numbers between one and fifty-six."

"That's interesting."

My grandma got up and walked to the door again.

"Tess, what I said in the car, about sleeping with more men, don't take any of that too seriously. I'd planned to shock you and win you over before we hit the Utah state line. Then I'd planned to correct much of what I said after we were well into Utah. But I didn't get that chance," she said. "Sex shouldn't be taken lightly. That was the point I was hoping to drive home." She clicked off my lamp and left the room.

I guess it made sense that somebody who had a capuchin-monkey-courtship strategy also had an interstate-driving-sex-education strategy. I was caught a bit off guard by her impeccable intuition. Somehow, my grandmother could sense that I was considering sleeping with Ben. I mean, my daydreams had barely begun entertaining it. Maybe Ben had let something slip in the car ride home from the hospital. Maybe Zena Crow was not the only clairvoyant individual in my life. Regardless, I tried to forget both my grandmother's comment and her sad, worried face. I tried to focus on Ben, the boy I loved and the boy who loved me.

I remembered him standing over me, telling me that he loved me. It had felt so good. The memory flooded over me, and I started to drift off to sleep. I hadn't taken any ibuprofen yet, but it didn't seem to matter. It was almost as if the sheer thought of Benjamin Easter and his love had the power to make all of my pain disappear.

Chapter 20

Christmas was uncomfortable, and there's not much else to say about it. Nobody thought of getting a tree or hanging up our stockings. Nobody had time to buy any presents. My grandma wrapped a can of black olives for me. But I didn't consider canned goods from the pantry, coated with dust, bearing a buy-one-get-one-free sticker, nearing the expiration date, a real gift. Also, they weren't the pitted variety.

We tried to have a formal dinner. My grandmother, parents, Ben, and I all sat around our table and ate lime Jell-O, green beans, canned beets, fruit cocktail, and my Christmas olives. By far, the worst part of the meal was the spongy ham, which my grandma didn't even pretend to like. Worse still, there wasn't much conversation. At least, not much polite conversation. It was so quiet that you could hear people chewing and swallowing and even breathing. It was like we were playing that game of who could be quiet the longest. My grandmother lost.

"Next time, buy the real thing," she said to my mother, poking at her meat with a fork, refusing to take one more bite. "This pressed stuff isn't fit for daily—let alone holiday—consumption."

"It was an economical decision," she said. "We all can't be lucky enough to have a cart full of money drop on our heads."

My grandma stood up from the table and took her plate to the sink. "I picked those numbers one by one," she cooed, scraping the majority of her meal into the garbage disposal. When she flipped it on, she neglected to turn on the tap water.

"It's designed to run with the water," my mother snapped, wringing her paper napkin so hard that it stopped looking like a napkin.

My grandmother turned on both of the faucets full blast. That's when Ben thanked my parents for the meal and excused himself from the table. That's when I dittoed his remarks and chased after him; my capuchin monkey days were long gone.

"I expect to see you back here in twenty minutes," my father called after me. My poor father. He had no idea that I no longer viewed him as the sort of parental figure that I had to consistently obey.

Ben and I climbed into his car and looked at each

other. I thought we were reading each other's minds. But I was wrong. I thought he was thinking about what a drag it was to listen to a severely dysfunctional family argue on a Christmas afternoon. But what he was actually thinking came out of his mouth in the following statement:

"Tess, I want to be alone with you."

I jokingly looked over my shoulder into the backseat.

"I want to be with you," he said.

"I have twenty minutes," I said.

Ben drummed his fists on the steering wheel in frustration, accidentally honking the horn. My mother parted the center of the living room drapes, peered out at us, and waved.

We waved back.

Ben set one of his hands on my thigh and rubbed it. My body felt electric and alive again.

"Why don't we go out this Friday night?" I offered.

"Tess, I think you're misunderstanding me. When I said that I wanted to be with you, I meant that I wanted to sleep with you."

I smiled and took Ben's hand.

"That's one idea," I said. "Will we rent a hotel room?"

Asking that made me feel extremely mature.

Ben shook his head.

"No. We should be somewhere special."

I jokingly looked over my shoulder into the backseat again.

"Tess, I'm being as serious as a heart attack right now."

"I'm sorry," I said. His posture was impeccably straight and he did seem quite serious.

I leaned over and kissed him on the cheek. I also accidentally honked the horn again with my elbow.

This time, my grandma parted the drapes and looked out at us. She could see that I was practically on top of Ben. She drew her finger across her neck, sending me the universal signal to cut it out. I slipped back into my own seat. Soon, my mother's and father's heads joined my grandmother's at the window. My father's was the highest head, just edging out my grandma's. My mother's head was the lowest, just poking up above the windowsill.

With only their heads showing, I really didn't see too many similarities between my mother's and grandmother's faces. If they'd have been in a lineup, I wouldn't have suspected that they were even related, let alone mother and daughter. But I did notice that their lips were making similar deep frowns. Then the drapes snapped shut, and I exited Ben's car.

I stood beside his driver's window, shoving my

hands into my coat pockets to keep them warm. The
air was cold and when we talked, white clouds floated
out of our mouths. We looked like we were smoking.
Of course, we weren't. Neither of us were interested
in paying money for a product that would give us bad
breath, turn our teeth yellow, and wreck our health,
possibly requiring us to lug around a tank of oxygen
in our twilight years, a time when we might already
be recuperating from hip-replacement surgery and
quite unable to heft the tank through the house, even
if it was on wheels, without the assistance of a paid
nurse or something. Ben spoke and blew out another
white breath.

"My parents own a cabin in Island Park," he said.
"We could go there. It'd be an adventure."

I had never realized how frightening it was to
make plans. I nodded. But then I remembered that
it was December.

"Is that place accessible by car in the winter?" I
asked. This time of year, I imagined that anyplace
so close to Yellowstone had to be swallowed beneath
twenty feet of snow. I imagined drifts higher than
telephone poles. Did he plan on snowmobiling
there? Because I knew I wasn't up for that much
adventure.

"The winter has been light and dry. Driving there
won't be a problem."

And so I nodded. And smiled. And nodded again. Ben started his car and backed out of my driveway. It didn't feel real yet. I wasn't sure I would go through with it. I turned around and ran back into my house, feeling overwhelmed, like I was on the verge of becoming a whole different person.

Chapter 21

I had one day to kill before the big event. Ben called once early that morning and suggested that we not see each other or talk again until tomorrow.

"We don't want to look suspicious," he said.

I'd never thought of that, but after he mentioned it, it was a hard thing to put out of my mind. When I ate my dry toast for breakfast, was I looking suspicious? When I started writing furiously in my journal, wandering from room to room, contemplating the rite of passage that stood before me, was that suspicious? When I stared for a good solid five minutes at my cast speculating on how my injury would impact my special moment with Ben, was that suspicious? I feared that it was, and went to my room. Surprisingly, nobody bothered me.

When I was in my room, I decided to read a book. I realized that after I'd started dating Ben, my book consumption had dropped off. Beside my bed was a pile of novels that Zena had passed on to me. She'd rated them as either four- or five-star experiences. And Zena was a discerning critic, so it was hard to hit that high on her scale.

I perused the five-star books. I didn't want to read *Pride and Prejudice,* because I'd already seen the movie and I was in the mood to get lost in a surprising new plot. I resisted picking up *Vanity Fair* because that thing was as thick as a Bible. And I wasn't drawn to *The Vet's Daughter* because, even though Zena had ranked it as a five-star double plus, something I'd never seen her do before, she'd also affixed a Post-it note to the paperback that said, "Brace yourself for a dead mother, animal cruelty, and a tragic levitation scene." I wasn't ready for any of that.

At the bottom of the five-star pile lay Edith Wharton's *Ethan Frome.* I figured that I was going to have to read it next year, anyway, so why not get a jump start? It was a thin book, something I was sure I could tackle in three hours. Right away I got the sense that I was reading one of the most important books of my life. It was a story within a story. It was also a mystery. I don't want to give everything away, but let's just say that three major happenings in the book really hit home: a broken pickle dish, a crippling sled accident, and unfulfilled love.

I felt like I was reading my own life, like if the moose accident had turned out differently, I could have been this miserable old guy named Ethan Frome. The thought of having my body disfigured or crippled stirred new fears inside of me. I always thought that the worst thing that could happen to a person was to be ambushed and eaten by a wild animal. Now I realized there was a whole range of horrible things that could happen to me that stopped short of death but robbed me of happiness. It was disgusting! A sixteen-year-old should not have to worry about that.

After I finished the book, I had a sudden need to look at myself, so I went to my full-length mirror. From my wrist to my shoulder my right arm was spotted with several softball-size bruises that were uneven shades of purple. My left arm probably had similar damage, but I couldn't see much due to the cast. I lifted up my shirt and looked at my chest. Above my Supra Bra was a deep pink circular bruise. It looked like the steering wheel had slapped me. I knew these things were temporary, but it reminded me of how fragile the body—my body—was.

I no longer had any doubts. It would be stupid for me not to sleep with Ben. I loved him. He loved me. What if something happened to one of us and we never had the chance to take our love to the next step? I started to cry. Not deep sobs or anything, but tears slipped down my cheeks and splattered onto my carpet. My face still had some bruising too. Beneath my eyes it looked like I was wearing blue eye shadow that had gotten smudged.

I didn't look horrible, but I was surprised that I hadn't taken total stock of my injuries until now. No wonder my grandma had been so weepy with me. Clearly, I looked like the victim of an accident. I lay back down and reached for another book. Ethan Frome had taken me most of the afternoon. I didn't have it in me to press on with another novel. For some reason, Zena had included a comic book about a pig with superhero powers; it fought crime mainly by swishing its curly tail. The pig was a woman, I think, because in several pictures it was wearing a skirt.

The superhero pig thwarted bank robbers several times by incapacitating them with powerful farts. And it stopped kidnappers by knocking them around with all four hooves. And it prevented a nuclear attack by eating the bomb before it could detonate. I couldn't believe this book was in Zena's five-star pile. But at the end of the book, she'd scribbled her reasons:

As a kid, I always wanted to look up to a female superhero who wasn't totally

*boobed out. Here she is. And look at her.
A flat-chested, flatulent, ridiculous pig
who will never find love or be taken
seriously. With so much sexist crap being
flung at us, how is a girl ever supposed to
turn out?*

Zena could be so deep. I closed the comic and thought of her in Arizona. I hoped she was adjusting to the heat. Then came a knock on my door.

"Tess, it's time to eat," my grandma said. "Pigs in blankets. Set your expectations accordingly."

She opened the door and looked at me. I guess I didn't look too enthused.

"I'm not a big pork fan either," she said. "But I don't mind bacon. Isn't it surprising that an animal can contain so many different tasting types of meat? A chicken tastes like a chicken. Period. Same thing with trout. But the pig, the pig has range, don't you think?"

"Are you sure they're not beef hot dogs?" I asked, rising from my bed.

She shrugged.

"I'm not a fan of the cow, either," she said. "Cows can cause a lot of misery. It was a cow that caused the 1871 conflagration that took Chicago. Mrs. O'Leary's cow kicked over a lantern."

"In history we learned that it wasn't the cow but a pipe belonging to some guy who was trying to steal milk from the O'Learys' barn to make booze. He confessed on his deathbed." My grandmother looked stunned, so I went on. "It took over a hundred years, but Mrs. O'Leary and her cow were totally absolved."

"You'd think they'd have put that on CNN," she said.

"I think they did," I said.

"Men and liqueur," she said. "They both can be a lot more trouble than they're worth."

I nodded, while thinking to myself, *But not my Ben.*

Chapter 22

My parents and grandmother gave me 100 percent approval to spend all of Saturday with Ben, because I gave them an excuse that was 100 percent bull. I told them that we were going to the library to work on a report about Isabelle Eberhardt, an explorer who lived extensively in Africa. She was born in 1877 in Geneva, Switzerland, but she died in 1904 in a sudden flash flood in the desert town of Aïn Sefra, near the Moroccan border.

Neither of my parents seemed to notice that this was the third major report I'd given on Isabelle Eberhardt in the past year. The first two were totally legitimate. One was for my sophomore social studies class and I focused on how Isabelle, an aristocrat, often dressed as a man in order to do nonwoman things such as explore. The second report I gave in my health class. The teacher had asked us to write a paper that answered the question "What's dangerous?" While I could have focused on the dangers of being a woman in the 1800s, instead I concentrated on the general danger of drowning.

At this point in my life, I was under the impression that sheer cockiness was the real reason that most people drowned. I knew that if you got swept into a fast-moving stream of water, the breast stroke, no matter how impressive your technique, wasn't going to be much help. I firmly believed that we should travel with life jackets stowed under our seats, much like the way airlines do it. I mean, how many times did we have to turn on the news and see a pickup truck being swept away by a swollen river before we caught a clue?

I think my reports on Isabelle Eberhardt opened up a lot of minds. Because in social studies, most people just gave reports on the same old explorers, the ones who killed hordes of people, but made way for us, so we didn't know whether to love them or hate them—like Cortez. And in health, I think I encouraged many of my classmates to think twice about neglecting to wear a life jacket.

So yes, I lied to my parents and headed with Ben to go to his parents' cabin in Island Park so that we could have sex. For me, it was going to be my first time. For Ben, it was going to be a higher number.

Yes, on December 27, I had sex with Benjamin Easter. And, yes, first-time sex is a big deal.

As we headed north on Highway 20, it was a somewhat stressful drive. My mind was spinning. I kept vacillating between whether or not I felt guilty about lying to my parents. In the end, I decided I didn't, because they'd freaking abandoned me for no good reason. I felt somewhat bad about lying to my grandma, but I knew she'd forgive me. Seriously, my left arm was broken and she owed me one. And I regretted that I hadn't called Zena to talk to her about my decision. But as of late, our relationship was a tad strained. I figured that I could catch her up on all the major events after I got back.

If there was one lesson she'd learned in all of this, I hoped that it was that you shouldn't build a bomb. Even though hers was just made out of fireworks and wasn't really a bomb at all, people still treated her like she had lost it and built an actual bomb. And then Ethan Frome popped into my brain. And the farting superhero pig. And Mrs. O'Leary's cow. My spinning mind thought about all these things.

Also, it thought about birth control and protection. I mean, I totally should have asked Ben if he'd brought a condom with him, but I didn't. I was too embarrassed to say that word. Which isn't a good thing. I mean, if you're ready to have sex, you should be able to say the word "condom." More than that, you should be comfortable enough to walk right into the drugstore and buy a big pack of them. Okay, maybe not a big pack. But before I could think much more about any of this, Ben broke the silence and interrupted my zooming mind.

"I'm thinking of a word. The clue is 'Indiana,'" he said.

"Gary?" I said.

"No."

"The next clue is 'house.'"

"Rambler?" I said.

"No."

"The next clue is 'airplane.'"

"Crap wad?" I said.

"No, that's two words. The answer is 'miracle,'" he said.

"That's deep."

He pulled off the highway and turned down a small road, heading east. After several curves, the road dipped and straightened and it felt as if we were driving down a bowling alley lined by tall pine trees. Before I knew it, Ben turned again, and parked his car in front of a snow-topped log cabin. We'd driven for an hour and a half, but it felt like nothing. I couldn't believe we were already there.

"This is it," he said.

The cabin looked cute; it was very triangular and had a dark green door and a cozy front porch with a swing on it. It was exactly what I'd imagined a mountain cabin would look like. Pine trees towered overheard, and from where I sat, I couldn't even see the tops of them. They stretched up past the clouds into the heavens and it was like witnessing something from *Jack and the Beanstalk*. Except it was more like *Tess in the Wilderness Amongst the Giant Pines Losing her Virginity Without a Beanstalk in the Vicinity*.

Looking at the gargantuan trees made me feel nervous. I knew I wanted to do this, but there was this little piece of me that thought maybe I should wait. But wait for what? I didn't want to be Ethan Frome. I was ready for my happy ending.

"What are you thinking about?" he asked. He put his arm around me and rubbed my back.

And before I had a chance to filter my answer through my brain, the little doubting piece of me won out and I blurted, "I don't know if I'm ready. I always thought I'd have a ring on my finger first."

Ben pulled his arm back.

"What?" he asked. He sounded nervous.

"I know that sounded stupid," I said. I buried my face in my hands. "I guess I'm old-fashioned." That's when I heard a bunch of jingling. Ben was maneuvering his numerous keys off of his key ring.

"Tess Whistle," he said. "I really like you and I see us being together for a long time. Even when I'm in college. You're special. One in a million."

Like an idiot, I thrust my casted arm toward him and the silver key ring. I knocked the keys out of his hand, and they tumbled into the crack between his seat and the center console. He laughed.

"No offense, but I think we need to use your right hand."

I extended my right arm and he slipped the oversize key ring on my fourth finger. Really, the whole ritual was stupid and corny, but it didn't feel that way at the time.

"Okay, now I've lost all my keys."

He pressed his hand into the crack and fished out key after key. I was quite relieved when I spotted that the car key had been located. Soon, his face was wrinkled with panic and he was digging with so much force that I could hear his fingernails scraping the carpet beneath his seat.

"What's the problem?" I asked.

"The cabin key," he said, pawing beneath his seat with both hands. Eventually, he got out of the car and moved his seat back. I did the same thing. It was so weird. It was like the key had been vaporized.

After about five minutes of looking, I started to get cold.

"Do you have a secret key hidden somewhere?" I asked. "Like in a fake rock?"

"No," he said. "I can't believe I lost it." Ben looked disappointed and angry. He repeatedly looked underneath his seat, as if he expected the key to re-form itself out of the floor mat and some mud clumps. I stopped looking altogether and turned my gaze heaven-ward. Maybe the big event wasn't meant to be.

Then Ben came up with a backup plan. He was very good at those. He opened his trunk and pulled out a sleeping bag.

"I brought this in case the cabin was too cold," he said.

I nodded.

"Sometimes we leave the back window unlocked. Maybe I can crawl in."

Ben seemed very determined to make this work. I wanted to make it work too, but to be honest, I was hoping to lose my virginity atop a quality sheet set. Not tucked inside a sleeping bag.

The window hadn't been left unlocked. The cabin was sealed up tighter than a walnut.

"Should we go back?" I asked. "It's cold out here."

"I have a better idea," he said.

And that's when Ben pulled me to him and gave me a deep, hard kiss, unzipped my coat, reached up under my shirt, and everything started to happen.

Chapter 23

I have to be honest. I felt dubious about losing my virginity outdoors. It seemed incongruent with who I was on many levels.

"Out here?" I asked.

"Under here," he said, pulling me toward the canoe.

"We could get hypothermia," I said.

"We so won't get hypothermia."

He kissed me again.

"Let's get underneath it," he said.

I didn't object. It was freezing, and I was ready. We quickly crawled under the canoe and began unzipping things. Once we were both horizontal, the slender boat created a quiet pocket for us. It actually worked much better as a sex shelter than I'd expected. Except for the temperature.

"Jesus, it's cold," I said, tugging down Ben's jeans.

"Forget it's winter. Let's pretend it's summer," he said, pulling off my coat and top.

I laughed.

"I don't think my mind is that powerful."

But I tried, anyway. I pictured us nestled on top of green grass, our feet bare, out fingertips warm, the air around us scented with wildflowers.

While I was losing my virginity, there wasn't much time for me to contemplate the act. It happened suddenly. One minute we were tearing each other's clothes off and kissing, the next we were inside the sleeping bag, naked. It didn't require a ton of effort on my part. It felt pretty natural. Although, I did feel slightly awkward with my cast. I tried to angle it off to the side so it wouldn't rub against Ben's back, because it was sort of itchy and I didn't want our first sexual encounter to leave him with a rash.

I don't know what I was expecting my first time to be like. There was some panting and moaning and kissing. That part was a lot like making out. Then came the moment. One second, I was thrilled and naked and excited by the idea of being closer to Ben. The next, I painfully felt him enter me. It wasn't unbearable pain, but it definitely was uncomfortable.

In addition to feeling him, I also think I felt the rubber. Ben, it turned out, fortunately had thought of bringing a condom. He said it was ribbed for my enjoyment, but I didn't really notice that. I was just relieved that he'd brought it. But I also felt stupid for not taking more responsibility. If things went badly, I would have been the one who got pregnant. And it's not like I was just having sex with Ben. There was his whole history to take into account. I was doing it with everybody Ben Easter had ever slept with and everybody they'd ever slept with. Exponentially speaking, it's like I was sleeping with a whole anonymous village. Just think of the potential risk factor for catching a disease!

After Ben and I had sex, he pulled himself out of me and things felt wet. I hadn't counted on sex being so messy and moist and I wished that I'd brought a towel. Ben kissed me again and again. On my lips. On my shoulders.

"How do you feel?" he asked.

"Good," I said.

"I'm glad."

I was quiet for a moment. Then I said, "How do you feel?"

Ben didn't answer right away. He pulled me closer, kissing the top of my head.

"Fantastic."

We stayed like that, Ben holding me, Ben kissing me, for about an hour. Then there was a definite chill, and we decided to head back. We got dressed inside the sleeping bag. Because of my cast, Ben had to help me quite a bit, and I accidently knocked him a good one in the head. When he lifted the canoe off of us, a cold gust of air somehow slipped inside my coat and chilled me to the bone. My teeth chattered as he led me to his car.

The drive back was longer than the drive there. I felt tired and wasn't very interested in making conversation, but it appeared that Ben had a lot on his mind.

"Remember when you asked me how much sex I'd had?" he asked.

"Yeah," I said, wishing I'd never asked such a stupid question.

"You're the second girl I've been with. The first was Valerie Geist."

"Oh," I said. I thought her name sounded boring, and I hoped that he'd stop talking about her immediately.

"She's my friend I told you about who has diabetes," he said.

I didn't say anything. I was too shocked by the irony of it all.

"With her, it wasn't about love. I mean, we didn't sleep together because we were in love. We were just friends."

I didn't say anything.

"I love you and I could feel the difference." He squeezed my hand.

"Why did you sleep with her if you didn't love her?" I asked.

He squeezed my hand again. "Last year, I thought I'd relapsed. At one point, before I got the test results, I just knew the doctor was going to tell me that he'd found cancer cells. When I was eight, I'd only had a month of treatment, and I always worried that they'd missed something. I thought cancer cells might have made it into my spinal fluid or organs. Even though the doctors told me I was fine, it was hard for me to believe that I'd been cured."

I watched the scenery fly past while Ben continued to talk.

"Last year, I was having night sweats and I got a nosebleed. I was so scared. I thought it was back. I thought I was going to die. Valerie was one of my best friends. She came over one night. One minute she was trying to comfort me, the next we were having sex."

I could see tears dripping off of Ben's chin, dropping onto his coat.

"I'm so sorry," I said.

"But I hadn't relapsed. And my parents ended up moving here to be closer to my grandparents. And

Valerie and I are still friends. But the times I was with her, it wasn't like this, Tess."

I decided to overlook the fact that he said "times," which was plural, which meant that he slept with a girl he didn't love repeatedly.

"I love you," I said.

Ben lifted my hand to his mouth and kissed it again. I didn't know what else to say to him. I really didn't want to talk about his cancer or hear anymore about Valerie Geist. Okay, I wanted to know a little bit more about Valerie Geist. She was part of the village and all.

"How long had you known her before you slept with her?" I asked.

"Years. We've known each other since second grade."

"Isn't it possible that she loved you?"

I could hear him breathing. He licked his lips.

"Maybe."

"Maybe!" I said. "You mean, you wouldn't know?"

"She never said she loved me."

I shook my head. That didn't mean anything. I decided not to ask any more questions, but I thought Valerie Geist probably did love him. I cupped my hands around my mouth and blew into them to warm them. Then I rubbed them together.

"Are you cold?" he asked.

"Yeah. Aren't you?"

"The heat is going full blast," he said.

"Good to know, but I'm relying on the power of my imagination." I pointed to my head. "In here, it's the middle of July."

"July, huh?"

"Yep."

"The cabin is gorgeous in July. If you want, I'll bring you up."

"Will we clock more canoe time?" I asked.

"You can count on it."

The miles ticked by. The gusting heat drained me and made me feel fatigued. The rest of the drive back, Ben held my hand and sang to the radio. An FM station was dedicating three hours to the Beatles. Ben knew all the words and sang along. I had never listened to the radio enough to learn the words to any songs. I didn't buy CDs or download MP3s. When I had extra spending cash, I liked to blow it on good books, comfortable socks, and frozen yogurt.

But I didn't mind the Beatles. Listening to their catchy songs, I thought about how sad it was that John Lennon had been assassinated by some stupid fan. Then, for some reason, I thought about John F. Kennedy, and that awful assassination. Then I blurted out, "I never want to name my son John."

Ben was quiet for a minute. Then he said, "I'm not really thinking about having children yet."

I think my comment made me look baby-crazy, which I was not.

"I'm not thinking about child conception or birth," I said. "I'm just thinking about names."

Then the Beatles started singing "All My Loving." They sounded so happy. I decided to interpret this as a good sign. I mean, the most famous band ever was singing our anthem. It was like even they supported what Ben and I had done, including the dead ones. Ben lifted up my hand and kissed it, and nibbled on my thumb.

"You even taste good, Tess Whistle," he said.

"Just don't take a bite," I said.

He pretended to eat my thumb. Then he laughed at himself.

"I've never had this much fun with a girl. Oh, I didn't mean it that way."

"I know how you meant it," I said. The thought of Valerie crept into my brain, but I forcefully shoved it out. Then, I reached over and turned up the radio and didn't really say anything else the rest of the way home.

Chapter 24

When I walked back into my house as a non-virgin, I felt like everyone was going to be able to tell what had happened, canoe and all. I hurried to my room and shut the door. It was then that I realized that I was missing the ring. I tried not to interpret this as a bad sign, like my union with Ben was destined to last for less than a lifetime or something. But the ring's disappearance did unsettle me. I decided to skip dinner. Sitting around the table with my parents and grandma was an event that I didn't mind missing. I heard my door creak open four times. I assumed that each of my parents came in once and my grandma came in twice. Needless to say, I didn't sleep like a rock. I drifted in and out, thinking about Ben and our future.

Waking up the next morning, the last thing I expected to see was a present. But there it was, situated at the foot of my bed. Even though it was wrapped, it was quite obvious that it was a book. Unless you really put your mind to it, disguising a book is not a simple feat.

It was big and heavy, and the gift tag said that it was from my loving grandmother. I tore it open and stared at an enormous book called *Our Bodies, Ourselves*. I didn't even need to flip open the cover and browse the chapter headings to figure out that this was a big book about sex. Even though I'd never heard of this particular book, it emitted strong informative-sex-book vibes.

My grandmother must have been lying in wait all morning. As soon as I'd finished peeling off the wrapping paper and crinkling it into a tight ball, she was at my door, nudging it open with each firm knock.

"Are you up?" she asked.

I looked at her and frowned.

"I don't want to talk about this with you right now, Grandma." I held the book so she'd understand exactly what I was talking about.

She stood in my doorway, tilting her head like she was confused. After flipping on my light, she continued to stare at me. I worried that if she looked at me long enough, she'd be able to discern that I'd slept with Ben. So I stood up and began pacing. I also tried to deflect suspicion by acting annoyed with her.

"I said I don't want to talk about it right now, and that's just the way it is." I continued to pace.

"What don't you want to talk about?" she asked.

When she started playing stupid, I no longer had to pretend that I was annoyed, because I'd actually become annoyed. I walked to my bed and thumbed open the book to chapter thirteen: "Sexual Anatomy, Reproduction, and the Menstrual Cycle." I stopped pacing and shook the opened book at her.

"I don't want to talk to you about sexual anatomy, reproduction, or my menstrual cycle," I said.

I could feel my face turning red and I wasn't sure if it was due to anger or embarrassment or lifting such a heavy book.

"Oh," she said, trying to sound surprised. "Okay. Your mother and I were getting ready to go to the mall. We thought you might want to come and pick up something for Ben, for Christmas."

"I do need something," I said.

"Why don't you come? You seem to have a lot of extra energy. And I'll sport you."

She handed me a hundred-dollar bill. Normally, I wouldn't have taken it so easily, but I needed to get Ben something.

"I have to shower first," I said.

"Okay," she said. "It's never fun to go shopping when you're feeling not so fresh." She flashed a smile and left my room.

Going to the mall seemed so harmless. I mean, I needed a gift for Ben, and the mall had so many stores to choose from.

We piled into my father's Buick Le Sabre and headed to the Grand Teton Mall. Harrison Q. Hart's survival camp had transformed my mother in many ways. She drove quite a bit faster than her normal pace. We had to be going at least fifty miles per hour, which was the posted speed limit on country roads.

"Are you thinking about buying him cologne?" asked my mother.

"No," I said.

"Are you going to get him a jacket?" asked my grandmother.

"No."

"Have you thought about giving him a subscription to a good magazine like *Time* or *National Geographic*?" asked my grandmother.

"No," I said. "But he does love marine life."

"Maybe you should get him Jacques Cousteau's biography. Or maybe you could save a whale in his name," suggested my grandmother.

"Maybe," I said. Until that point, I'd had no clue that you could save a whale in somebody else's name.

In fact, it wasn't totally clear to me how you went about saving a whale to begin with, other than not harpooning one.

We got to the mall, and my mother parked her car extremely far away from the entrance.

"Walking is good for the heart," she said.

"But icy parking lots are bad for the butt," my grandma responded.

I laughed. Then I cautiously chose my steps, avoiding numerous patches of ice, all the way to the front door.

Once inside the mall, I became a total wanderer. My mom went off to Sears to look at shoes, and my grandma headed to the Book Rack. I thought about getting Ben a shirt. Or a stuffed animal. Or pants. But none of that seemed important enough. We were having sex; I had to get him the perfect gift. Then I saw a sign made out of yellow neon posterboard that really grabbed my attention: black bears $6. I knew that was false advertising, because there's no way on God's green earth that anybody could sell a black bear for six lousy bucks.

I followed the yellow neon signs all the way to Big Ark Pets. Inside, there were birds yapping, puppies whining, fish swimming, and tarantulas feeling their way up glass walls. I didn't see any bears.

"Can I help you?" asked a young, oily-faced boy, very near my own age.

"Where are your black bears?" I asked.

"You're in luck. We only have one left."

He led me to the cash register. There, in a wire mesh cage, sitting in a pile of cedar chips, crouched a plump black hamster.

"They're bred to be docile, but if you wake this girl up from a nap, she will bite."

I think he could tell that I was disappointed, so he let loose some hamster trivia.

"Hamsters have eighteen toes. Four on each front foot and five on each back foot. They're nocturnal, which means that they sleep during the day, so I wouldn't keep her in your bedroom."

The hamster looked at me and twitched her nose.

"You wouldn't want to put a boy hamster in with her. Hamsters have the most compressed reproductive cycle of any mammal. I mean, in terms of non-egg-laying or marsupial mammals."

"Oh," I said. I wasn't totally sure what a marsupial mammal was.

"But if you do want to breed her, once she has babies, you'll want to get the male out fast. If you had a Chinese dwarf hamster, you could let the father stay. He'd actually help with the rearing of the young by bringing the mother food and even keeping the babies warm when she went out to stretch her legs. But dwarf hamsters will breed again within twenty-four hours!" The clerk shook his head back and forth and put his hands on his hips. "Also, the mother may eat the babies. I know, it seems absolutely wrong, but it happens."

"That's disgusting," I said.

"Yeah. Also, keep in mind that the average litter is about seven, but could be as high as twenty-four. That's the maximum number of pups that a hamster's womb can contain. Twenty-four," he repeated, opening and closing both hands, flashing me twenty fingers, then opening up one hand again, keeping his thumb tucked under, flashing me another four.

"But this isn't a pregnant Chinese dwarf hamster, right?"

"Right, it's a black bear hamster."

"How did you learn so much about hamsters?" I asked. I mean, he acted like he'd graduated summa cum laude from Hamster University.

"Oh, my girlfriend gave me my first hamster and I fell in love with it. By the way, if you buy a hamster, you really ought to get this book."

He handed me a thick pamphlet with a lime green jacket that said *Fifty Important Things You Should Know About Your Hamster*. A golden hamster was showcased on the front; it appeared to be smiling, revealing two humongous teeth.

I took the book and stared at that cute little black hamster sitting near the cash register, squatting contentedly next to a metal wheel, puffing his cheeks.

I think it was impossible for me to miss the symbolism of purchasing a *black bear* hamster for Ben. I mean, a black bear hamster. Ben had helped me overcome my fears of wild animals, bears in particular. And if I gave him a hamster, Ben would be forced to think about me every time he fed her, or held her, or changed the water, or cleaned the cage. (Okay, I really didn't want him to think of me while he cleaned her cage.)

When it struck me that he would have to take the hamster to college with him, and tell everybody that his girlfriend gave it to him, I realized I had to buy her. So I bought her. And a cage. And a water bottle. And a ceramic food dish. And food. And that pamphlet. And everything else Craig, the hamster brainiac, suggested. And while I was checking out, I spotted a coffee mug that said I HATE YOUR POODLE. I think it was intended as a purchase for people who owned dog breeds that they felt were superior to poodles, but it also worked well as a gift for Zena. So I bought it.

I met my mother and grandmother at the Yogurt Lab, hamster and gear in tow.

"You bought him a rodent?" asked my grandmother.

"When did you become so impulsive?" asked my mother.

"She's for Ben," I said. "It's the perfect gift. I know he'll love her."

"A hamster is a far cry from marine life," said my grandma. "Other than for drinking, they're not even supposed to come into contact with water. They bathe themselves with sand and their own body oil."

"My word," said my mother. "How do you know so much about hamsters?"

"I read," said my grandmother.

"Tess, is that a coffee mug? Are you drinking coffee now? That's so much unnecessary caffeine. And what do you have against poodles?" asked my mother.

"They are kind of yappy," I said.

My grandma smiled at me. Neither of them appeared very impressed with my purchases. But I didn't care. I knew it was the perfect gift for Ben. And I was sure Zena would think the mug was hilarious. At least I hoped so.

Chapter 25

After the acquisition of the hamster, my life began to unravel at breakneck speed. First, before I was able to give Ben his hamster, Zena called.

ZENA: "I'm sorry I yelled at you and hung up on you. I've been going through a hard time. Thanks for your letter. And the fifty bucks. But I didn't buy Twizzlers. I've given up refined sugar. It triggers mood swings. And no, my boobs are both the same size."

ME: "It's good to hear your voice. That's great about the sugar. And your boobs. How are you?"

ZENA: "I'm feeling better. Robert's called a couple of times. He's coming back home in May. My parents say I'll be coming home sooner than that."

ME: "That's great. So what's going on with your dad and Mindy?"

ZENA: "He broke up with her. He and my mom are attempting a reconciliation."

ME: "What about Dr. Tong?"

ZENA: "He's out of the picture."

ME: "Is he dead?"

ZENA: "No. He moved to Belize."

ME: "Why?"

ZENA: "He snorkles."

ME: "Oh. I have news."

ZENA: "Is it about your car?"

ME: "No. The car was totaled when I hit a moose heading south on I-15. I mean, I was heading south. I think the moose was stationary and grazing."

ZENA: "Are you okay? That's how Sheila Stadler died, you know."

ME: "I broke my arm, but I'm fine. But that's not even the news." I took a deep breath. "I slept with Ben."

ZENA: "No way. Drive me to the hospital and give me a CAT scan. I am talking to Tess Whistle, aren't I?"

ME: "Listen, frozen airplane waste ripped through a house in Indiana. It was like a sign. And I'd hit that moose. And Ben is a cancer survivor. And I read *Ethan Frome* and it made me realize how you're not young forever and your sleigh could hit a tree. I mean, life is short, Zena. And I love him."

ZENA: "That's so intense. But I think you misread that story's message. And I thought you wanted a ring first. Wow. I wish I could have been there. Well, not there there. I hope you used a condom. And even if you did, unless it's put on correctly, you still risk getting pregnant or catching a disease. And remember, sometimes they break."

ME: "Well, it didn't break, and he's had sex before. He knows how to use a condom."

ZENA: "What do you mean he's had a lot of sex?"

ME: "I didn't say a lot of sex. He's just had some. He slept with his friend Valerie Geist after he thought his leukemia had relapsed. He didn't love her. But I think she might have loved him. She was a diabetic. Anyway, that doesn't even matter. I bought Ben a hamster today and we're doing fantastic."

ZENA: "So much has changed with you— broken arms, sex, rodents, leukemia."

ME: "I'm exactly the same person."

ZENA: "Are you sure? Sex didn't change you?"

ME: "Of course I'm sure. Why, did sex change you?"

ZENA: "No. Not so much. Wait. My aunt is knocking at my door. I've got to go. I'm running late for yoga. You should try it. It's very centering. Plus, it increases your flexibility. Ben will appreciate that."

ME: "Don't make fun of me."

ZENA: "Tess, remember to break for moose. I'll call again soon."

Then she hung up. She didn't even really say good-bye. Then my grandma knocked on my door and I told her to go away because I was preparing the hamster's habitat. I heard her footsteps moving away from my door.

I thought I should set up the rodent's home so that when I gave it to Ben, it was already up and running. I sort of liked this little hamster. She kept twitching her pink nose at me and rubbing her paws against her face, like she was washing herself without any water. I didn't try to hold her because I was intimidated by her front teeth. For a finishing touch, I put a bow on the cage and carried it into the bathroom so that I could fill the water bottle. I decided to leave the assembled habitat in there, because it had a smell to it. Then I called Ben.

ME: "Is this Ben?"

BEN: "Why, were you looking for Cautious Bob?"

ME: "Oh, I'm always looking for Cautious Bob."

BEN: "Ha-ha. Tonight he's got a segment on rabid racoons."

ME: "Yeah, I've seen that one. It's actually very informative."

BEN: "You watch a lot of Cautious Bob."

ME: "I watch some. Moving on, let's play *Password*. The clue is 'habitat.'"

BEN: "'Jimmy Carter.'"

ME: "Why did you guess Jimmy Carter?"

BEN: "He helps build houses for Habitat for Humanity."

ME: "The guy who used to be president and liked peanuts?"

BEN: "Yes, why—is the answer a different Jimmy Carter?"

ME: "No. You got it right. It was Jimmy Carter."

In the end, I decided that I really didn't want to play *Password* with my Christmas present. So I told him to come over for a surprise. He said he had something for me, too.

Ben had perfect timing and arrived while my parents and grandmother were out at the grocery store buying the fixings for supper. Nobody wanted a repeat of Christmas dinner. I guess that last night they each ordered their own pizza, as nobody could reach a decision on the toppings.

When I opened the door and let him in, I threw my arms around him and he gave me a deep kiss.

"I have something for you," he said.

"I have something for you, too."

"I want to give you what I have first," he said.

I didn't argue. Ben reached into his pocket and pulled out a small box. He pulled the lid off, and inside sat a small silver ring with a milky white pearl in the center.

"Oh, my gosh," I said. "It's a ring."

"Smart girl," he said. The ring was tucked into a fold of gray fabric that looked like a pair of concrete-colored lips. Ben pulled the ring out and slipped it on the fourth finger of my right hand.

"It's a promise ring," he said. "It means I want to be your boyfriend indefinitely."

"That sounds like a long time," I said.

He leaned in and kissed me. "It will be, unless you contract rabies from a rabid racoon."

I snapped the box shut and swatted Ben on the shoulder. "Don't even joke about that. I think I was almost attacked by a raccoon once."

"You mean you're not sure?"

"It was dark. I was camping in Yellowstone. We'd spent all day looking at geysers, fumaroles, and mud pots and were camping in Upper Coffeepot, because all the campsites inside the park were full."

"What's a fumarole?"

"It's a dry geyser. Basically, it's a hole in the ground without enough water to be a geyser, so it sizzles and hisses and smells like a rotten egg."

"I'm surprised you didn't devote your whole trip to solely looking at fumaroles."

"Stop joking. This is serious."

"Okay, you were camping in Upper Coffeepot."

"Like I said, it was dark and I was walking to the latrines and I heard some rustling up ahead off the trail."

"Maybe it was somebody who preferred bushes to latrines."

"No, I had my flashlight. So I whipped it out and flooded the area with my lightbeam. That's when I saw its masked bandit face. And I'm pretty sure it was foaming at the mouth."

"Did it try to attack you?"

"No, I ran straight to the toilets and slammed the door. But anything could have happened. I hear that they're excellent at launching ambushes."

"Racoons? I'll start packing mace."

He was laughing, and this really ticked me off because I can clearly remember that night, that racoon, and my enormous fear.

"Listen, it could have been rabid. And if I were you, I wouldn't start carrying mace. In the majority of cases, unless you really know what you're doing, your attacker finds a way to use it against you."

He burst out laughing.

"Given their resources and skills in ambushing, I'm surprised racoons haven't taken over the earth."

"Okay, I wasn't talking about racoons anymore. You know what I meant."

Ben pulled me to him and give me a strong kiss.

"It sounded like a traumatic incident. I didn't mean to laugh."

"Yes, you did," I said, pushing him away.

"Well, I didn't mean to laugh that hard."

He pulled me back toward him and kissed me again. I felt his hands untucking my shirt and reaching under my blouse. Ben and I walked up to my bedroom, and even though I was a little sore from yesterday, we did it again, in my bed.

The second time, I felt a little more comfortable with my body. I didn't worry so much about my cast or the fact that my breasts were not the same size. I think it took a little bit longer too. It's such a weird feeling to have somebody else inside of you. Even if you love him.

After he was finished, we hurried to put our clothes back on, because my family would be home any minute. Ben noticed the book about sex.

"That's one big sex book," he said. "Does it come with diagrams or suggested positions?"

"It's not that kind of sex book. My grandma gave it to me."

We heard the door open and the sound of an argument.

"I don't want to stay for dinner," Ben said.

"But I have something for you."

I pulled Ben into the bathroom and drew back the shower curtain.

"It's a black bear hamster," I said.

Ben didn't say anything at first. He looked at it like he wasn't sure if it was actually alive.

"Is it a stuffed animal?"

The hamster lifted herself onto her back legs and licked at her water bottle.

"Does it have a battery inside it?" he asked.

"No. It's totally alive! You can take it to college. It'll be like you're taking a piece of me with you."

"College is nine months away. What's the life span of a hamster? Will it live that long?"

"Yeah, but you have to feed it fresh fruit and vegetables for maximum life span. What's wrong? Don't you like her?"

"It's a girl?"

"Yes, and you need to name her."

She rubbed her paws against her face again and twitched her nose.

"Lincoln," he said. He smiled at me and moved toward the hamster's cage.

"Lincoln was a man and he was assassinated," I said.

"Lincoln can be a girl's name. I mean, it is just a hamster, Tess. And it's a real compliment. Lincoln is a great historical figure."

"I've always wanted to name my kids after presidents, but none of the ones who were assassinated. That's too weird."

Ben picked up the cage and bit his lip.

"Why are you talking about kids again? Tess, you're sixteen."

I felt so stupid. I didn't actually want to start having kids. I had no idea why I kept bringing them up.

"Naming her Lincoln is totally creepy," I said.

"Tess, this is my present. You gave her to me. She's my hamster."

Soon, my parents and grandmother were in the hallway with us.

"Good to see you, Ben," said my grandma. "We're having fish tacos tonight. I hope you'll join us."

"I can't," he said. "I promised my mom I'd be home for dinner. I just came to exchange presents with Tess."

I flashed my pearl ring at my grandma. My mother and father caught a glimpse of it too.

"Wow," said my grandma.

"A ring," said my father.

"I didn't realize things were so serious," said my mother.

"Well, you have been away," added my grandma.

Ben took the cage and the information pamphlet and headed for the front door.

"I'll call you later," he said.

"That was a swift exodus," said my grandma.

"You're really too young to be getting a ring," said my mother.

"Did you buy your boyfriend a rat?" asked my father.

"No!" I yelled. "That's Lincoln the black bear hamster. I'm not in the mood for fishy tacos!"

I turned on my heel and went to my room, slamming the door so they understood that I wanted some privacy. I decided to open up my sex book and do some reading. That's when I learned about my hymen. I guess that's why I had a little bit of blood in my underpants. Reading about breaking it after the fact, I felt a sense of loss. I lay in bed thinking about my unforgettable week. After I was through rewinding the last seven days in my head, I heard a soft knock at my door.

"I'm just not a fan of fish or tacos," I said.

"What about gerbera daisies and purple Matsu-moto?" my grandmother asked.

She opened the door and walked in holding a large bouquet of bright flowers.

"Are those from Ben?" I asked. *He really must have loved that hamster,* I thought.

"Better," she said. "They're from Zena."

"They are?" I was so excited that I jumped up and started smelling them. "They're gorgeous."

"The girl has taste," my grandma said. "She didn't go for the regular old roses and alstroemeria combo. It's lovely."

My grandma set them down on my dresser. She angled them so I could see the arrangement perfectly centered from my bed.

"There's three notes," she said. "I think you have to pay extra for three, so I'd appreciate them to the fullest."

"I will," I said.

My grandma left without saying anything else.

"Are you tired?" I called after her.

"Only of certain people," she said.

I think she meant my parents, but I try not to get involved with that. I leaned over my flowers and took another deep whiff. They came just in time. The smell of onions and frying fish was drifting into my room, and Zena's flowers seemed to act like a fish-odor repellent.

First note: Sorry to hear about the moose. Sniff these and get well.

Second note: When done properly, sex should be about your pleasure too.

Third note: These cost way more than fifty bucks. I don't regift. Even money. I miss you.

Due to the graphic nature of note number two, I hid all three between my mattress and box spring. I never ended up going downstairs for dinner. And Ben never called me. I hoped he didn't try to go to sleep with Lincoln in the room. Because she was nocturnal. Which meant she'd be up all night running in her squeaky wheel. I sure hoped that Ben was reading his information book. Tonight, I drifted off to sleep thinking about Zena. The notes seemed spunky. And in our last phone call she'd seemed like her old self again. I wanted her back home soon.

Chapter 26

The end came quickly and I never saw it coming. I woke up the next day feeling a little down. First, the big excitement was over. I hadn't been a virgin for two days. And the guy I'd lost it with seemed a little ticked off at me. Which I didn't even think was fair, because it was weird to name your pet after an assassinated historical figure.

Second, my best friend was living in the desert, restructuring her life with the assistance of her therapist aunt. And her return date was, as yet, undetermined.

Ben didn't call all morning. I went downstairs and had breakfast with my grandma. My parents were upstairs packing, preparing to leave again for Utah. They planned on celebrating New Year's at the survival camp.

"Are you enjoying the book?" she asked.

"Yeah," I said, chewing my toast. "But I don't want to talk about it."

"Okay," she said. "It's not the sort of book that you read from cover to cover. You should utilize the index."

"Yeah," I said.

"So how did Ben like his hamster?"

I set my toast down and looked my grandmother right in the eye. "I think it caught him off guard."

"Living animals often do."

"I should have saved a whale in his name."

"There's always Valentine's Day."

And when she said that, for some reason I was overtaken by this gloomy feeling and a sudden need to call Ben.

"Tess, can I ask you a question?"

I lowered my head. I didn't want to be asked a question.

"Sure," I said, avoiding eye contact.

My grandmother pulled out a framed picture of a man.

"Why did your parents have a picture of Harrison Q. Hart underneath the couch? Do you think this guy is some kind of cult leader? A Jim Jones?"

I shook my head.

"That's not Harrison. It's Jesus, Grandma."

My grandma stared hard at the picture. "A blonde?" she asked.

"It matched the couch," I said.

My grandma walked the picture to where it belonged and hung it on the nail. "It's better than a cake pan," she said.

I agreed. Then I went upstairs and called Ben.

All he wanted to talk about was how often Lincoln went to the bathroom.

"Frequent urination could be a sign of a disease," he said.

"Read your booklet," I told him. I had no idea that this suggestion would doom our relationship.

Ben didn't seem all that excited to talk to me. He seemed distracted, so I got off the phone. I didn't get a chance to read more of my book, because my parents wanted me to help them load their car and say formal good-byes.

"We'll be back next weekend for a visit," she said. "Remember, your grandma is the captain of the ship."

My grandma saluted my parents from the front step. I kissed them both good-bye. We babbled on about how much we were going to miss one another. Deep down, I was secretly hoping that like Zena's parents, mine would snap to their senses and return to normal. (Be careful what you wish for.)

I watched the tires grind through a fresh blanket of snow and pull out onto the open road. My grandmother and I both waved. Then I returned to my room and she headed to the grocery store, rattling off a lengthy complaint about my mother's shopping habits, which she felt relied too much on canning technology.

"What's wrong with buying beans and leafy greens?" she asked, picking up her purse.

"I think they make her gassy," I said.

"Once you eat them enough, the body adjusts. And hasn't she ever heard of Beano?"

Then, she was gone. After the accident she'd decided to rent the next car, a big white Ford, I'm not sure what kind. It had the appearance of an enormous rectangle.

I went upstairs and watered my fabulous flowers. Seven orange petals had already fallen from some of the gerbera daisies, but the purple Matsumoto was still standing strong. I flopped on my bed; my mind stuck like a broken record on all thoughts related to Benjamin Easter. I wondered if he was going to go to college closer to where I lived. I wondered when we were going to start having babies. Three years? Four years? I wondered when I was going to talk to him again. So, very unlike a capuchin monkey, I called him a second time.

He ended up coming right over. I'm not sure why we had sex again. I think it was because we could.

Neither one of us was that into it. It wasn't thrilling like the first time. Or adventurous like the second. When we were finished, Ben rolled his body away from mine. I played with his curly hair, then drifted off to sleep. When I woke up, he was dressed again, leaning down to kiss me good-bye.

"Are you going?" I asked.

"Your grandma will be home soon. I don't want her to think that we're sneaking around and ban me. She's already giving you materials related to sex education."

"Ban you? Maybe you should go." He kissed me and was gone.

I decided to make some brownies. They were going to be the pecan caramel kind from a box. But we didn't have eggs. So I called my neighbor, Mrs. Kirby, and walked next door to borrow some of hers. And while I was there, Tess Whistle's happy life fell apart.

I was only at my neighbor's for about ten minutes. She gave me the eggs right away, but then she wanted to show me all of her holiday cards. She's a widow and she had a bunch of them. As I was walking back home, I knew that something was up, because Ben's car and my father's car and my grandma's rented Ford were all parked in the driveway. It looked like a caravan.

I walked into my house carrying the two borrowed eggs, one in each hand. My mother looked like she'd been crying. My father looked confused. Ben looked angry and a little bit like he'd been crying too. My grandma looked pale.

"You've got some explaining to do," my mother said.

I was so worried that they'd found out that I'd been having sex that I dropped the eggs on the tile entranceway and they cracked right open.

"Why did you lie to me?" Ben asked.

I had no idea what he was talking about.

"I haven't lied to you," I said.

"Then when exactly were you diagnosed with diabetes?" my mother asked.

My mouth fell open. I didn't have anything meaningful to say.

"I'm so sorry. It wasn't a lie so much as it was a total accident," I said to Ben.

He shook his head. "I'll call you when I'm ready to talk."

He walked out of the house and slammed the door.

"What's going on?" I asked my parents.

"They've decided to stay," my grandma said. "And turns out that you bought Ben a diabetic hamster. He came over to borrow some testing strips. Your parents had just gotten back, and I wasn't here yet. So they fielded that one."

"Why would you tell such a lie? And don't claim it was an accident," my mother said.

I turned to my grandma. "What should I do?"

"Wait for him to call. Then explain yourself."

I could see the keys to my grandmother's Ford tucked into the outside pocket of her purse. I grabbed them.

"I think I can fix this," I said, bolting from the house.

Everybody ran after me, but I didn't care. I made it to the car and sped away. It was like I was fleeing from the scene of a crime. My crime. My own stupid unforgivable mistake.

Chapter 27

I drove immediately to big ark pets and spoke with Craig the hamster brainiac. He told me everything I needed to do in order to test Lincoln's urine for diabetes.

"You could have mentioned that the hamster might have been diabetic," I said.

"Usually it only happens in dwarf hamsters. I'm very surprised by this news," Craig said.

"Well, that makes two of us."

I tried to be as nice as I could and not take out all my frustrations on Craig. I mean, this was more my fault than his.

Then I had to drive to Fred Meyers and visit their pharmacy and load up on test strips that were designed to test both ketones and glucose. I also went to the pet section and bought some sugar-free seed mix. Craig had been very clear about the need to monitor a diabetic hamster's sugar intake. He reminded me four times to sort Lincoln's food and remove corn and peas from the mix. And he repeated three times the importance of keeping all fruit out of the hamster's diet as well as any treats that include sugar in the ingredients.

I showed up to Ben's house literally weighted down with diabetic hamster supplies. Luckily, neither of his parents was home. I had to knock on the front door and ring the bell several times before I got any response. When Ben finally opened it, he said that he wasn't ready to talk.

"I know. I'm worried about Lincoln. I brought what you need."

Reluctantly, Ben let me inside and led me back to his room.

"You really shouldn't try to sleep with Lincoln," I said.

"What?" he asked.

"I mean, you shouldn't try to sleep in the same room with her. She's nocturnal."

I smiled wide. Ben looked away. I reached into the cage and pulled out the hamster.

"You can leave this stuff. I can do it on my own."

"No, let me help," I said.

That's when Lincoln decided to slip inside my sweater. I'm not sure if she intentionally burrowed her way into my cast, or if she slipped inside. It was a tremendously odd feeling to have a live animal trapped against my skin.

"Hold still," Ben said, lifting my cast upward, trying to tilt the hamster out.

I shook my arm. I jiggled the cast. At some point, Ben retrieved a wooden spoon and inserted it inside my cast.

"Don't poke it," I said. "You'll kill her."

"Relax," he said. "This is outrageous."

"I'm thinking of a word I said. The clue is 'rabid.'"

"Don't."

"I'm so sorry, Ben. You might not believe me, but I promise that I'll never lie to you again."

"Stop. I'm not ready."

Finally, Lincoln darted out of my cast and ran straight into Ben's lap.

"That's fantastic!" I said.

"Tess, please go home."

I was in shock. Ben led me to his front door. He swung it open and held it that way with his outstretched arm. That's when I noticed a mole on his wrist that I'd never seen before. I couldn't believe it. That mole looked exactly like the profile of Abraham Lincoln.

So I blurted it out. "Your mole looks like Abe Lincoln, the picture of him on the front of the penny."

"It's a birthmark," he said.

"Whatever, don't you think it looks like Abraham Lincoln?"

"Not until your grandmother pointed it out."

Then I had a thought that didn't sit well with me.

"Did you name our hamster after your mole?"

"Lincoln is my hamster, and it's a birthmark."

I leaned in to kiss him good-bye, but he pulled back.

"I said that I'm not ready."

He shut the door. I heard the latch catch in the backplate. But I didn't hear him lock the dead bolt. I took that as a sign that his heart was still somewhat open to reconciliation. I released an audible sigh of relief.

That's when I saw it. The symbol of my broken dream. The tangible evidence of my derailed life. The canoe. Our canoe. It was strapped with bungee cords to the top of a minivan. I couldn't believe it. What was it doing here? It belonged at the cabin. Ben and I had plans to go back there in July, when everything would be warm, green, and lovely. We were going to fool around underneath it in our shoeless, sockless feet. He told me that I could count on it.

I don't remember shrieking the word no, but I must have, because Ben quickly swung the door back open.

"What's wrong?" he asked. "You sound like you're being attacked."

Probably, I should have concocted a second lie and told him that I'd been attacked by a random dog that had just left. But I chose to be honest instead.

"The canoe," I said. "What's it doing here?"

"My parents are giving it to my aunt Charma and uncle Sam. They're going to patch it and paddle it around Lake George," he said.

"And you're letting them have it?"

"It's not my canoe."

"And you're okay with this? Isn't Lake George in Utah?"

"Yeah. And yeah."

I blinked several times, hoping he'd say something else. Something more meaningful.

"But it's more than just a canoe," I said.

"I guess," he said. "I mean, I know."

I watched his gaze settle on the upside-down, tethered boat. We were both quiet.

"Tess, being sick—having a diagnosed medical condition—that means something to me—"

I didn't let him finish. I jumped right in.

"I know. That's why I'm here. Because I understand."

Ben shoved his hands into his pockets and looked down at his shoes. I reached for him, but he turned his body away from my touch.

Then he looked up at me. He was biting his bottom lip and his eyes were filling with tears.

"No," he said. "You don't."

And by the tone in his voice, I knew he was right.

Then he was gone. I stood there looking at his front door. Then I turned and clapped my eyes on the canoe again. It was all so sad. So out of my control.

As I drove back to my house, I didn't even worry about what kind of trouble I was in. I had lost Ben. That was the worst punishment I could imagine.

I pulled into my driveway, and all three of my parents ran out onto the front step.

"This is unacceptable," said my mother.

"I won't tolerate this," said my father.

"What a pickle you've made," said my grandma.

I felt like I was dead. Nothing mattered. I thought that I'd never eat again. I thought my life was over. My parents sat me down on the couch and informed me that they'd decided to stay. They apologized for running off. But Harrison's camp had equipped them with new and necessary tools to survive in this ever-changing world. Now my parents wanted to work on everything. On their marriage. On their relationship with me. Even on their relationship with my grandma.

"Does this mean you're staying?" I asked my grandma.

"Probably not," my father said.

"Tess, why did you tell that boy that you had diabetes?" my mother asked.

"I don't know," I said.

"Lying is a dirty habit," my mother said.

"We all make mistakes," my grandma said. "It's not like she killed the president. Look at her. She regrets what she's done. She looks horrid."

Everybody stopped to stare at me.

"Tess, go take a nap," my father said.

So I dragged myself upstairs, where I made another stupid mistake. I think I waited ten minutes before I called Ben. When he answered, I was so happy, I started to cry.

"Tess, I'm not ready."

"But I want to know about Lincoln. Does she have diabetes?"

"Yes," he said.

"I'm so sorry."

Ben didn't say anything.

"I'm sorry about everything," I said.

"Tess, please, stop calling."

"Happy New Year," I said. But he'd already hung up.

So it was over. The boy I lost it with had left me with nothing but a dial tone. My parents came to check on me several times. My grandma brought me a pitcher of ice water and some paper cups.

"You've spent a lot of tears over this. Stay hydrated or you'll get a pounding headache."

All night long, I thought of Ben. I don't know why I never told him that I didn't have diabetes. I don't know how that lie got so big. In the beginning, it was so small, just something to keep me from feeling embarrassed. How it turned sinister, I'm not quite sure.

I hadn't eaten much. I wasn't hungry. I just kept sitting by the phone waiting for Ben. Around lunch, my grandma came in and told me that she had a good feeling about how all this would end. I hoped she was right.

"Deep down, you're a good girl. Ben knows that."

I positioned myself by the phone so that I could answer it if it rang. It had only rung once, and it was a woman for my mother. She sounded so happy, and it was annoying to me that she couldn't detect by the tone in my voice that she was talking to somebody whose world had just ended. Her optimism wounded me. I'd never realized that one person could assault another person using joy.

Hours went by. No Ben. No Ben. No Ben. Maybe I'd left the phone off the hook. Or maybe it was broken. I checked it. The phone was working fine. I decided to use reverse psychology and intentionally leave the phone off the hook. I figured this might encourage him to call. It seemed like it could work.

My door opened. I'm not quite sure why people had ceased making a courtesy knock before entering. Before me stood my grandmother wrapped in a baby blue towel.

"Your parents have gone to a French restaurant," she said. "Contemplate what kind of pizza you want. After I get out of the bath, we'll order it."

"I want to go back in time and change things," I said.

"My dear, time only moves in one direction. You should read a book," she said. "Or listen to some music. The Mormon Tabernacle Choir always lifts my spirits."

"Are you kidding?" I asked.

"Absolutely not. Studies have shown that organ music can quicken the heart."

"That doesn't prove anything. Maybe the people in the studies were fans of organ music. I mean, what demographic were they testing, anyway? Senior citizens living in Utah?"

"Well, that's food for thought," my grandma said. She left my room and returned with a chocolate bar. "If it's that time of the month, chocolate may help."

"Grandma, I have a question."

"Shoot."

"How did Bismarck die?"

"Otto von Bismarck, the Iron Chancellor of

Germany? He lived to be eighty-three. I assume it was natural causes."

"I meant the capuchin monkey."

"Well, that's a sad story," she said.

"I didn't expect it to be funny."

She planted an arm on her hip and looked up at my ceiling, as if she were transporting herself back to the exact moment he expired.

"It was the Fourth of July. I was eleven. There was a big picnic at our house. My grandma and grandpa Tucker were there. That's your great-great-grandma and great-great-grandpa Tucker."

I nodded.

"Well, Grandma Tucker was bound and determined to kiss that monkey. Bismarck's leash was tethered to the ground by a railroad tie that had been driven into the grass. All day long, Grandma Tucker tried to sneak up on Bismarck. She'd even tempted him with pieces of cantaloupe. Finally, after we'd eaten, Grandma leaped toward Bismarck."

"Did she kiss him?"

"No, Bismarck jerked so hard to get away that he yanked the railroad tie clean out of the lawn and darted with his leash into the street."

"Did he escape?" I asked.

"No. He was struck by a cement truck."

"And killed?" I asked.

"Instantly. I think the lesson from this story is obvious."

"It is?"

"Yes," she said. "First, sometimes it's best to respect a monkey's personal space. Second, if you bring a pet monkey to a barbecue, always secure him to a sturdy tree. Third, it's unpatriotic to pour concrete on our nation's birthday."

"I guess I see a different lesson."

"Oh?"

"First," I said, "playing hard to get is a risky game. Second, people really shouldn't own monkeys. Third, aggressive women run in our family."

"Well, that's what happened to Bismarck. He was such a sweet and intelligent monkey."

"He got hit by a truck. How's that intelligent?"

She left again and returned with a second chocolate bar. Then she exited my room for good. The pipes groaned as she drew her bath. I held back tears. I didn't mean to be a vehicle for bitchiness, but it was so hard to control my feelings when I was wallowing in a pit of total despair. I'd made such a mess. What was I supposed to do? What did Ben expect me to do?

Chapter 28

It's been three days since I've talked to Ben. I keep thinking that he's going to call and say, "Tess, I forgive you." But Ben may never forgive me. It's New Year's Eve, maybe he's waiting until tomorrow so we can start the year fresh.

In honor of New Year's, my parents have gone out to dinner. Actually, this is the third night in a row that they've gone to a French restaurant and left my grandma to take an exceptionally long, skin-shriveling bath. While she's in there, I blare the Mormon Tabernacle Choir. It's not like I'm on a religious jag. I play their greatest patriotic hits CD. I like hearing the symbols crash.

It's dusk. I'm looking at myself in the mirror. The bruises underneath my eyes have turned yellow. I look like I have a disease. On the bright side, I think something about intense traumas reduces the bacteria that causes zits. I haven't had any in weeks.

I wonder what would happen if I called Ben. I wonder what he's doing for New Year's. I wonder if I drove by his house and looked through his windows if I'd be able to see what he was doing. I wonder if he drives past my house. If I sit by my window, I wonder if I can see the road clearly enough to catch a glimpse of him if he happens to drive by.

I walk to my window expecting to see some snow falling or maybe the moon. But when I open my curtains, I do not see snowflakes or moonlight. I see a face. I see Zena Crow!

"I'm back!" she yells into the closed window, her breath a white cloud blooming between us.

I'm too stunned to say anything. I unlatch my window and lift it open. It's freezing outside. My room is on the second floor. After reading a story in fourth grade about the frequency of house fires, I demanded that my parents hang an escape ladder from it. While I've never considered it sturdy enough to climb, Zena has never had a problem scaling its aluminum rungs.

She slips the screen off. My parents really should use storm windows; it would cut down on our winter heating bills. Zena flings the screen down and it drops onto the snowy ground.

"You could have handed it to me," I say.

"That thing was filthy," Zena says, holding up a pair of white ski gloves smeared with two thick lines of grime. "It's probably carrying the plague. You don't want it in your bedroom."

"Why didn't you use the front door?" I ask. "Have you run away?"

"No. I'm home now. And I knocked on the door and nobody answered. I've been calling since noon, but it rings busy."

"It's off the hook. I'm using reverse psychology," I say. "And I didn't hear the doorbell because I'm listening to music."

"I noticed," Zena says.

After she climbs in my room, she unplugs my stereo. Then she gives me a big hug.

"It's so good to see you," she says.

I break into tears.

"It's good to see you, too," I say.

"What's wrong?" she asks.

"I miss Ben."

"Ben?"

"Yes, Benjamin Easter. He dumped me."

"Do you think he was only after *one thing*?" Zena asks, narrowing her eyes.

"I do," I cry. I bury my head in my hands. "Honesty."

Zena slaps me on the back. "Show me some spine," she says. Zena is wearing a backpack and she takes it off and sets it on my floor. "Ooh, look at the flowers. Sometimes they really don't give you what you pay for, but these are exactly how I imagined them. Don't you just love orange gerbera daisies?" She lightly taps some of the petals and smells her finger.

"I want him back. Do you have a plan?" I ask. "Are you going to help me? Maybe I can somehow become a diabetic. Maybe I can somehow convince him that I've been a diabetic the whole time and that this was a total mixup."

"He only likes girls who have diabetes? That's not normal, Tess. Does he suffer from some sort of mental disorder that you're not telling me about?"

"No, he mistakenly thought I was a diabetic," I say.

"That doesn't make any sense. Why would he think that?"

"I sort of told him that I had diabetes and now he knows the truth and he hates me."

"Well, he probably doesn't hate you."

"But he doesn't love me anymore. He doesn't want to see me. He's asked me not to call."

"Tess, some guys love it when girls play hard to get."

I fall to the floor crying.

"I know. That's why I acted like a monkey."

Zena stands over me.

"Did you ever fake going into insulin shock?" she asks.

I stop crying and look up at her.

"No."

"That's good. It shows that you have clear ethical boundaries when pretending to suffer from a serious illness."

"I really do," I say. "Now you just need to help me come up with a plan to get him back."

Zena shakes her head. "This isn't *Days of Our Lives*, Tess. You can't scheme your way back into somebody's heart."

I'm crying again. Zena retrieves a copy of *Ethan Frome* from her backpack and I break out into sobs.

"Not that book," I say. "That thing totally misled me."

Zena wraps her arms around me. "You're going to be okay. You told a lie. Ben will get over it. Things will work themselves out."

"By tomorrow?" I ask. "Tomorrow is New Year's. It would be so appropriate to forgive me by tomorrow." Snot runs from my nose onto Zena's shoulder.

"That's not likely," Zena says.

"Next week?" I ask.

"Tess Whistle, you are going to be okay whether Ben gets over this or not. If he can't forgive you, it says a lot more about him than it does about you."

"Oh, my God! I have it. I know how to fix things," I say.

Zena puts her hand on her hip and doubtfully scans me up and down.

"I can start a letter-writing campaign and bring *Password* back to television. It's his favorite game show."

Zena blinks at me several times.

"Or maybe you could call NASA and see if they've got room on the next shuttle. I mean, isn't it every boy's dream to fly a rocket into outer space?"

"No, I'm serious. This could work. He loves *Password*."

"Okay, if you can get the Fair Winds Senior Living Center on board with your letter-writing campaign, it should only take you about five years."

"That long?"

"Tess, *Password*'s already on television in reruns. It's on the Game Show Network."

"Yeah, but Ben wants to be a contestant on the actual show. I could make it possible. It's like one of his biggest dreams."

When I say this, I stretch my arms upward, to emphasize the dreaminess of what I want to do.

"Is that a hickey on your neck?"

I cover my neck with my hands. "You're so crude. I like to think of it as a love note."

Zena rolls her eyes. "Earth to Tess. It's a patch of skin Ben sucked too hard."

I let my arms drop beside me.

"*Password* isn't going to work, is it?" I ask.

"No."

"I shouldn't have lied." I break into sobs again and dive onto my floor.

"Have you started taking the pill? Are your hormones out of whack?"

"No, I'm not taking the pill. According to *Our Bodies, Ourselves*, the best form of birth control is the barrier method," I say.

"You mean not getting naked?" Zena asks.

"No, you know, a diaphragm. A cap for the cervix. And a condom, of course."

"You've come a long way. You bought a diaphragm?" Zena asks.

"No, but I was planning on making an appointment to get fitted for one," I say. "Soon. And purchase some spermicidal jelly." I lower my head into the carpet and start crying.

"Good God, Tess. Get a grip." Zena hands me a pair of ski gloves and a hat. "Put them on."

"But I don't know how to ski."

"We're not going skiing."

I decide to trust Zena. Luckily, the gloves are extra large and fit over my cast. I slip them on. I'm getting tired of feeling crappy and helpless. Some activity would be a vast improvement.

"My parents are out to dinner. My grandma is taking a long bath."

"Leave a note," Zena says.

And I do.

> Went out for fresh air with Zena.
> Love, Tess

"Do you think Ben is missing me too?" I ask.

"Tess, I love you. Please lay off the Ben references for a few minutes. Desperation doesn't become you."

"I never should have embraced that capuchin monkey strategy. I should have stayed honest." I almost start bawling again, but Zena hurries out the door and I don't have time to break down. We get in her car, and she drives to the top of Iona Hill.

"This is where Ben helped me overcome my fear of black bears," I say. Tears slip down my cheeks and land in patters on my coat.

"Bears are extremely dangerous; you can't reason with them and they have intolerably bad breath. I'd retain some fear in that area."

Zena pulls on her emergency break. Below us the lights of Idaho Falls twinkle like a Christmas village.

"Living with my aunt, I learned a lot. I understand

why I built the bomb. I understand why I acted out. I think I understand why you're an absolute puddle at the moment too."

Zena turns to face me. She puts her hand on my knee.

"It's okay that you slept with Ben. Unless you're like a nun or something, nobody stays a virgin forever. It's okay."

"But I feel like I lost something."

"After the excitement, after the actual moment, I think that's the way it's supposed to feel. For a little while."

I cry and nod.

"It's something we all lose."

"I should drink Diet Coke. Why didn't I drink Diet Coke? It was the apple juice." I double over and put my face in my hands.

"Okay, you baffled me earlier with your capuchin monkey reference. This Diet Coke and apple juice stuff isn't helping."

I hold back my tears and sit upright. I tell Zena how it happened. How the stuff in my locker clobbered him. How I was embarrassed. How I liked his butt. How it was the first time I'd ever even noticed a guy's butt. How the lie seemed so small, almost like it was nothing and then got bigger and bigger and then I didn't know what to do.

"Okay," she says. "Once he wants to talk to you
again, you can explain all that to him, minus the butt
obsession. Seriously, he's not a Neanderthal. He'll
listen to you. Eventually, he'll become reasonable.
Right now he's just upset."

"You're a good friend," I say, sniffling hard. "I
didn't even know purple Matsumoto was a flower
before you sent me some."

Zena hugs me.

"You're a good friend too."

"I feel stupid. I feel sad."

"Give it time. You'll feel better."

I sniffle. Zena doesn't seem to understand that I
want to feel better right now.

"You're clairvoyant. How do you think Ben feels?"
I ask.

"I don't know," she says. "I never use my powers
to spy."

"You don't?"

"I'm a big believer in karma and I don't want to
get bit in the butt."

"Don't say the word 'butt.' It makes me think of
Ben."

Zena climbs out of her car and opens the trunk.
She keeps the lights to her Mercury on, and I see that
off to the right there's a sled path. Zena hauls out a
red plastic saucer sled.

"I think you need to complete a life metaphor," she says.

I get out of the car and stare at her.

"You're crazy," I say.

"No, I'm not."

She looks very stern. Then I realize, due to the poodle bomb, my comment was a tad insensitive.

"Okay, you're not crazy, but this is a bad idea," I say.

"It's a fabulous idea."

"I could break my neck," I say.

"You're not going to break your neck. The hill isn't that steep."

"What if I hit a tree? You read *Ethan Frome*." My tears are gone now. Snow is softly falling and I'm blinking furiously.

"There's only one tree."

She points to a large pine that's at least twenty feet to the side of the sled path.

"It only takes one tree!" I say.

"Have some faith," she says.

"Where does the trail end?" I ask.

"Right there," she says, gesturing to a long, flat area at the bottom of the hill.

"Are there rocks?" I ask.

"I've seen toddlers sleigh down this."

"Were they wearing bicycle helmets? I mean, head injuries are pretty serious."

"Tess, you need to learn how to let go."

Zena and I stare at each other. I think she may be right.

"While I was in Arizona, my aunt made me write down all my problems on bricks. Then she had me throw my bricks into a pool. Then she had me retrieve them. Then, using a sledgehammer, she had me pound them into pieces. It made so much sense and made me feel so much better. It was a life metaphor. I was angry, and I got that anger out of me."

"Well, I could do that," I say.

"Anger isn't your problem. This is what will help you."

"I'm not sure," I say.

"Trust me. I gained insight into my behavior."

As Zena talks, I can feel some of the old Tess coming back. "But your aunt is a licensed therapist and you're just Zena."

"Thanks," she says. She sets the saucer sled at her feet. "Come here."

"I don't get how this is supposed to work. Shouldn't I yell something while I'm going down the hill?"

Zena smiles at me.

"Like what?"

"Maybe I should confess a regret or something."

"I like that," says Zena. "Very cathartic."

But when I see the hill's sharp slope, I hesitate.

"What's wrong now?" Zena turns my body to face hers.

"I just remembered a segment Cautious Bob did about jagged rocks hidden beneath snow near sledding hills." I turn away from her and look down the hill.

"You're not telling me you still watch that goon?"

"Not every night." Looking at the hill, I'm overtaken with nostalgia. "When Ben brought me here, we made out. We kissed and he held me. In addition to bears, he helped me overcome my fear of coyotes, too. And wolves."

I feel like I'm going to cry, but instead I feel an icy wetness slap across my face. I turn to Zena. Her left hand is holding a snowball. Her right hand is empty.

"What was that for?" I ask.

"A reality check," she says. "Get on the sled."

I shake my head. Zena hurls another ball my way. It crashes into my stomach.

"Stop assaulting me with snow," I say. "It doesn't feel good."

"Tess, some things in life are out of your control. You lied to Ben. The ball is in his court. Your virginity is behind you. You need to look to the future. And yell that thing about a regret."

I take the sled and walk to the path. But the only

thing I can see is that tree. What's Zena thinking? What if I hit it? I take a deep breath.

"It's a big tree," I say.

"It isn't anywhere near your path, Tess. If you're always worried about hitting the tree, you're never going to get down the hill."

I know she's right. I sit on the sled. Zena's headlights illuminate where the trail ends, but beyond that, before the city starts, there is a cold, dark nothingness. That's what Zena wants me to descend into.

"So what is your biggest regret?" Zena asks.

"I thought I was supposed to yell it."

"Whatever. I was trying to make a moment."

"I regret hurting Ben and also killing that innocent moose."

"Really? Do you regret the moose thing more than the Ben stuff?"

"No, but the moose is dead. I feel like I should include it."

"That's true."

"And the moose was a lot bigger than Ben."

"I imagine it would have been."

"It was enormous. A couple of times I've worried that it might have been pregnant. What if it was? What if I'm responsible for the demise of two moose? That's, like, an entire moose generation."

"While I'm glad to see that you're using this moment to dig deep, the idea was to release a regret, not obsess over it. Besides, your grandma sent me a newspaper article and it reported that you killed a bull moose weighing 1,200 pounds. It's highly doubtful he was expecting."

"It's a relief to know that," I say.

"Are you ready?" she asks.

"Wait, I have something more to say about my moose regret."

"Okay."

"I knew it was a bad idea to drive in the snow. I felt like something bad was going to happen. But I ignored it. I should have waited for the snow to stop. The moose would still be alive."

"Or somebody else might have hit it," Zena says. "Freeways, snowstorms, and grazing moose are a deadly combo."

"Maybe." I feel a lump in my throat. I swallow hard to get rid of it. "I never meant to hurt anyone."

"I know," Zena says.

"Wait, I think I should say something positive about myself, too."

"Is this a stalling tactic?" Zena asks.

"Not at all. I don't want to shoot down this hill focused entirely on my screwups."

"Okay, yell something positive, too," Zena says.

"Yeah, but I'm not sure what I should say, and my underwear is really riding up and it's hard to concentrate when you have a wedgie."

I try to turn my head and face her, but she is directly behind me. "Actually, I don't think I even need to do this," I say. "I slept with Ben in a sleeping bag outdoors in Island Park. I think I'm at peace with the unknown."

Zena puts her hands squarely on my shoulders and draws me and the sled back to her.

"No offense, but it sounds like that whole situation was a series of his decisions and not yours."

"No, it's what we both wanted. I really liked him."

"But think about it. You lied to Ben about the apple juice to manipulate his opinion of you. You wanted to control what he thought of you. But some things are beyond your control. Tell me. Why did you always want a ring before you slept with a guy?"

"I don't know."

"Tell me."

Tears are forming behind my eyes. "I guess I wanted to make sure he loved me."

"Tess, you wanted a promise—a guarantee—that he would never leave you. But you can't guarantee the future. A ring doesn't do that."

"It means something," I say.

"Did you hold out for a ring?" she asks.

"Sort of. He gave me a nice pearl ring for Christmas," I say.

"That's my point. You still have the ring, but you don't have Ben."

I am about to agree with some of what she's said, when I feel her shove me. It isn't hard, just enough to launch me forward. Wind and snow strike my face, but I don't close my eyes. I'm going downhill. I safely pass the tree. The sled makes a scraping sound as it glides over an icy patch. Everything feels like it's moving very fast, but really, other than the tumbling snow, I'm the only thing in motion. Due to my high rate of speed, I forget to yell anything. It's like I'm in flight.

It's New Year's Eve and the lights in front of me are so distant that even as I grow closer, they seem very far away. Besides Zena, nobody knows that I'm speeding down this hill. Snow stings my skin. I keep my eyes open the whole way. Once I'm at the bottom, the sled rocks to a stop. I roll off and trudge back up the hill. Zena is hopping at the top, flashing me a victory sign. It's nice to have a friend who's willing to be such a cheerleader. Literally. What exactly is she cheering? Wait, she's not cheering. She's screaming, and tumbling down the hill, right toward me.

I guess this makes sense. You really shouldn't jump up and down on the lip of a snow-covered hill.

Instead of moving out of Zena's way, I reach out to slow her down. I grab her coat as she zooms by. But she's moving too fast. I'm tugged back down with her, clinging to her sleeve with my good hand.

Snow swats us as we somersault down the hill. The snow conforms to fit inside my ears, up my nose, around my ankles, and down my back. I'm so glad I'm wearing tight pants, because I get the feeling that this slushy stuff can worm its way into any orifice. We finally crash to the bottom. Zena lands on top of me across my legs.

After we both take a moment to catch our breath, she scoots off of me. I sit up and look back up the hill to the car. Our tumultuous descent has churned the deep snow into a rough-looking mess. We look like we've plowed the path.

"Are you okay?" I ask.

"Yeah. Are you?"

"I think so," I say.

"Do you feel better?"

I nod and try to shake some snow clumps from my hair.

"I do."

I stand up and pull Zena to her feet. I throw my arms around her, almost knocking her back down. I'm so lucky to have her. Friends like this only come around once in a lifetime. I know this.

"Thank you," I say.

"Anytime," she says.

Over her shoulder, I look out at the valley. In the bowl of lights beneath us, my parents are eating dinner, my grandmother is bathing, and Benjamin Easter, the boy I love, is out there too, doing something. I've hurt him. Things are out of my hands. This may not end up how I'd hoped. I let go of Zena and turn to walk back up the hill with her. As we near the top, her headlights catch us, casting long shadows behind us. We look thin and exaggerated, like we're several stories tall. From the right angle, I bet we look a little bit like superheroes. I toss the sled in the trunk and climb into her car.

"I'm so cold," I say.

She turns the heater on full blast, but it blows nearly the same temperature as the air outside.

"Imagine that it's summer," she says.

Zena doesn't know that I've already been there and done that.

"I'm finished with mind games," I say.

Zena nods and disengages the parking brake, then carefully steers us back down the hill. Perched at a stoplight, her heater begins belting out warm air. I cup my hands around a vent and lean in close. She smiles at me. Not with her mouth, but with her gold-flecked green eyes. I've missed those eyes. I smile back.

Zena flips on the radio. The Beatles are singing "We Can Work It Out." The song is nearing its end. I'm tempted to interpret the lyrics as a sign. But it's probably just a coincidence. As Zena drives, the station fades out. But that's okay. For the first time in a long time, I feel hopeful. And ready for what comes next.

HUNG UP

March 1, 11:25 a.m.

This is Lucy calling to update my order BKE-184. Looks like I won't need the leather strap after all. So, just to be clear, keep the rest of my order as is, but cancel the strap. Thanks!

March 5, 3:11 p.m.

It's Lucy again calling about my order BKE-184. Is it too late to rethink materials? In the end, recycled aluminum just sounds cheap. I'd rather go with the slate. All the reviews I've read say that slate will endure both heat and snow better. Plus, it has more effective results for tree attachment. Thanks for working with me. Can you please call me so I know you got this order change? My number is 802-555-0129.

March 6, 4:10 p.m.

It's Lucy. I called yesterday about order BKE-184. Nobody has gotten back to me. Please let me know that my order has been updated. Natural slate plaque. No leather strap.

March 8, 10:04 a.m.

It's Lucy calling about order BKE-184. I'd like confirmation that you received my requests for an order change. I'm worried because you still haven't called me back. I'm not high maintenance, if that's what you're thinking. I'm not going to modify anything beyond this point. I understand that you have strict shipping dates. If you're upset about my leather strap cancellation, just go ahead and ignore it. I'm willing to eat the cost on that. I really want to know when you plan to ship my order. I'd also like to remind you that I've already paid in full. So I deserve a return phone call. I mean, I don't like threatening people. But I also don't like being jerked around. My number is 802-555-0129. You better call it.

March 15, 11:38 a.m.

Lucy: This is the last message I'm going to leave before I call the Better Business Bureau—

James: I'm speaking. You're not leaving a message.

Lucy: When are you going to ship my order?

James: I'm not.

Lucy: You have to! I paid for it.

James: My name is James and you haven't paid *me* anything for anything.

Lucy: Not cool, James. I paid somebody in your company.

James: I don't own a company. You're about the thirtieth person who's—

Lucy: Do I have the wrong number?

James: Not exactly . . .

Lucy: This sounds like a total scumbag operation.

James: No. There is no *operation*. My name is James Rusher. I'm a senior at Burlington High School. I'm not connected to this plaque/trophy/crystal awards business in any way. It's my cell phone. I just got it. I took a recycled number. I guess I got a deadbeat trophy company. I'm sorry to tell you this, but I think they've gone out of business.

Lucy: That sucks. I mean, I can't believe this is happening.

James: Um . . . It's not exactly the end of the world.

Lucy: Easy for you to say. What are my options here? What am I supposed to do about my order?

James: I guess you order another slate plaque without a leather strap from a different company?

Lucy: You know, you could pretend to have some sympathy. I've been robbed.

James: You're right. I'm sorry. You sound nice. I feel bad you got taken. The guy who ran that business sounds terrible. He even ripped off people who'd ordered gravestones for their pets.

Lucy: Wow.

James: I hope somebody catches up with him and makes him pay all these people back.

Lucy: Yeah. Okay. Thanks. I'll let you go.

James: Lucy, I bet with enough effort you can find this guy. It's really hard for people to just totally disappear.

Lucy: Um. Yeah, I'm pretty busy, and I have zero interest in playing detective, James. I think I'm just going to accept that I got screwed.

James: Your call.

Lucy: Yeah. It is. Okay, good luck with midterms.

James: How do you know I've got midterms?

Lucy: You said you go to Burlington High.

James: Interesting. And do *you* go to Burlington High?

Lucy: No, I live in Montpelier. I have a friend who goes to Burlington High.

James: Who?

Lucy: I'm not going to tell you my friend's name. You're a stranger.

James: Is it your *boyfriend*?

Lucy: I'm going to hang up on you, James.

James: Don't hang up.

Lucy: Stop being obnoxious.

James: No promises there. It's how I'm built.

Lucy: Are you going to call back all the people who are leaving you messages about this company?

James: I don't have that kind of time.

Lucy: You don't feel obligated?

James: Why would I feel obligated?

Lucy: Well, they're calling you.

James: I've got midterms to study for, remember?

Lucy: Okay. I'll let you go, James.

James: You're fun to talk to. You can call me anytime.

Lucy: Thanks. But I'm probably not going to do that. Bye.

March 17, 4:18 p.m.

James: Hey, Lucy, it's James. You called me last week about your plaque and leather strap. I told my friend Jairo about your situation. He says he knows how to get that stuff wholesale. Shoot us the dimensions you want, and he thinks he can get you what you need. Let me know if this works for you.

March 19, 5:52 p.m.

James: Hey, Lucy, Jairo can't fill your order. He got hit in the head with a tree limb today. Don't worry. He'll be okay. We tried to start a company using the disgruntled client base of the deadbeat trophy company. Not the people with outstanding orders. Those people are out of luck. But we figured we'd take the new callers. And this woman needed us to measure her mailbox, because she wanted a new address plaque. And it was near a tree. And Jairo underestimated his strength. And he shoved her quaking aspen. And a limb fell and totally nailed him. Looks like we won't be taking that job. Anyway, I've been doing some sleuthing, and I think I have the home phone number of the now-defunct trophy company. I've been giving it out to people who call me with outstanding orders. It makes me feel like a cross between a private investigator and Robin Hood. Also, I feel a little bit like a bounty hunter. But don't worry— I don't own any weapons. Except for baseball bats, hockey sticks, stuff like that. And I only use those to play sports. Hey, this is a long message. And it's starting to sound weird. Sorry.

March 20, 3:30 p.m.

Lucy: Hi, James, that's too bad about your friend's head. From what I hear, quaking aspens can be very brittle and unpredictable. Mature ones can crush a bystander to death. It happens all the time. Well, maybe not all the time. Yes, give me the deadbeat plaque maker's home phone number. Also, it surprises me a great deal that you (a) consider a hockey stick to be a lethal weapon, and (b) feel a little bit like a bounty hunter. Have you ever seen a bounty hunter? I have, on TV. They're usually overly tattooed and pretty rough looking. Plus, they have mullets and violent tendencies. Is there something you should tell me?

CRIMES OF THE SARAHS

Just like mayonnaise, Raisinets, and milk, every criminal has a shelf life. Either you get caught or you evolve. Much like the amoeba, the other Sarahs and I plan on evolving. Of course, since we're in the middle of a job right now, we're obviously not there yet.

"Should I go?" Sarah B asks.

I view this as a rhetorical question. I'm not the leader. That's Sarah A's position, but she's already inside the store. Sometimes, because I'm the driver, when Sarah A is absent, the other two Sarahs defer to me. Though I don't know why. Among the four of us, I'm the least alpha. I'm not headstrong or decisive or anything. As far as the pecking order, I'm the shortest Sarah. Plus, I struggle with anxiety.

"Give her a few more minutes," Sarah C calls from the backseat.

Had I said something, that would've been my answer too. I always favor inaction over action. Sarah B leans back into the passenger seat and smacks her gum. Then she blows a bubble so big that its circumference eclipses her face. *Pop.* She peels off the pink film and pushes the gum wad back inside her mouth. Bubbles never stick to Sarah B's face, because every minute of her life, her T-zone is aglow with oil. It's what I call a Teflon complexion. Except I don't say that to her actual face. *Pop.*

A fact that sucks: Sarah B breaks out more than any other Sarah. Another fact that sucks: Her oily skin will age better than my dry skin. When she's eighty, her skin will be the least wrinkly of all the Sarahs. That is, if we all live long enough to reach that geriatric benchmark.

"Now?" Sarah B asks.

I shake my head. It's not just that I favor inaction; in the beginning, we learned quickly that it was best to enter our targeted stores one at a time. It's blatantly unfair, but salesclerks absolutely stereotype teenagers. Even a group of presumably innocent, Caucasian-looking, female teens browsing the aisles of a bookstore on a Sunday afternoon can send up a red flag. Agism is alive and well, even here in Kalamazoo.

"Now?" Sarah B asks me again. "I feel like it's time."

I nod. I don't know if it's time, but there's so much tension and perfume overload in the car that I'm getting a headache and it would improve the atmosphere immensely if the apple-scented Sarah B left.

"Remember, take the clerk to the board-book display

through the strip mall parking lot, her brown hair bouncing around her tan, bare shoulders. Until last week, Sarah B always wore a Detroit Tigers baseball cap. But after she almost got caught shoving a box of Oreos down her pants at a Sunoco station, Sarah A was adamant that the cap had to go. She claimed that the bill shaded Sarah B's eyes, making her look boyish and deceptive.

Sarah A was the only Sarah who saw it this way. Sarah B has very big boobs. There's nothing boyish going on with that rack. But immediately following the Oreo incident, while we sat around Sarah A's bedroom indulging in our looted booty, Sarah A grabbed the cap right off of Sarah B's head and doused it with lighter fluid. I was really surprised that an incoming high school senior kept lighter fluid in her bedroom. Then, Sarah A ran to her bathroom and torched the hat in the tub. At that point, the cap became a moot point.

But we've all moved on from the flaming cap episode. That's clear as I watch Sarah B bounce right through the front doors of the Barnes & Noble. But what else would I expect? She's a resilient Sarah. We're all resilient Sarahs. So while it may be true that we've reached a criminal level of boredom with our city, to the point where we've considered committing much more serious crimes with actual weapons, we're still a very plucky bunch.

"I'll go in ten," Sarah C calls from the backseat.

She's the only Sarah among us who had to legall

beneath the huge toad cutout. Ask a lot of questions about Sarah Stewart and David Small. Keep the clerk in one area," Sarah C says. She's leaning forward, wedging herself into the rectangle of open space between the driver's and passenger's seat. Her shiny red hair is so close to my mouth that I think I can taste her conditioner.

Sarah B opens the car and slings her purse strap over her neck. For as long as I can remember, Sarah B has feared being mugged. I guess being a thief lowers your threshold for trust.

"I thought it was a cutout of a lizard," Sarah B says.

"He's a toad," Sarah C says.

"How do you know it's a guy? Is it anatomically correct? Did you inspect its crotch?" She blows another bubble and sucks it back inside her mouth.

"First, he's wearing pants. Second, he's a character from *The Wind in the Willows*. It's a guy toad. Trust us."

Sarah C kicks the back of my seat.

"Yeah, *The Wind in the Willows* is about a male toad," I say.

Sarah B tilts her head and squints at us, like she's thinking really hard. Her soft lips turn downward, which usually means that she's confused.

"I bet some cultures consider lizards to be a form of toads," Sarah B says. "They both have reptile brains." Not everything Sarah B says makes perfect sense.

She slams the car door and enthusiastically walks

change her name. It wasn't the easiest thing to do. She and her parents had to petition the family division of the circuit court and pay almost two hundred dollars. Sarah A made Sarah C bring the paperwork to prove she'd done it. Because if you're going to become part of an elite club, there's got to be some standards. Sarah A was very clear about that. So, our freshman year, Lisa Sarah Cody became Sarah Lisa Cody. A bona fide Sarah. For the most part, she doesn't seem to regret it. But who wouldn't want to be one of us? The benefits are stellar. The Sarahs are popular, crafty, goal-oriented, and have loads of unsupervised time. My parents aren't expecting me home for hours. And when I do show up, it's not like they'll pepper me with probing questions about my afternoon. A few years ago, after I joined the school choir, they assumed I was on a good path in life. I look like a good girl, and around them, I act like a good girl. Which is cool. I may be passive, but I do care what people, especially blood relatives, think about me.

"Hey, don't you ever worry that we'll get caught?" Sarah C asks.

She finger flicks the back of my head. I rub the area and keep my hand there to shield myself from a second flick.

"Are you speaking hypothetically?" I ask.

"No, like right now. Don't you worry some hyper-aware clerk will spot us?" Sarah C asks.

"That's not what I was thinking about at all," I say.

"Even if we do get caught, I guess it's not a huge deal because we're minors. We'd probably be sentenced to make restitution and pick up roadside trash. But after we turn eighteen, we might want to rethink this lifestyle."

"Lifestyle?" I try to glance at her in the rearview mirror, but her head is tucked down. "This is more than a lifestyle. It's who we are. We're the Sarahs."

"Yeah, I know, but once we're eighteen, once we're in college, we should probably rethink it. I mean, theft is kind of immature. We want. We take. Is it really worth it?"

"Of course it's worth it. Look around. We've got a close circle of friends and a ton of free crap."

Sarah C leans forward again. This time she angles her body so she can face me. I don't look at her.

"But doesn't all the free crap ever weigh on your conscience?" she asks.

"My what?"

Sarah C lowers her voice to a whisper.

"Sometimes, I picture myself handcuffed. Actually, I imagine all four of us in handcuffs, being trotted out to a squad car, the lights flashing, broadcasting our guilt to everybody driving by."

Sarah C mimics a siren by emitting a *wha wha* sound. Then she puts her hand over her mouth to dim the noise.

"Stealing stuff all the time is a lot like driving a race car," Sarah C says. "Drivers are warned not to look at the wall when they're losing control, because you tend to steer yourself toward what you're looking at. For criminals that's a very appropriate life metaphor: In order to avoid colliding with the cops, don't think about them."

"I never think about the police," I say. Neither the topic of law enforcement or car crashes strike me as positive pondering.

"Besides the Sarahs, what do you think about?" Sarah C asks. I don't like her tone; it's accusatory. Or her question; it's a little too insightful.

"I think about life," I say.

Sarah C leans into the backseat again, but this time threads her long legs through the center console. Her sandals reach the gearshift. I get the feeling that she doesn't believe me. She crosses her ankles and I watch her toes curl incredulously against the brown suede pad of her shoes. I feel goaded into elaboration.

"I think about life all the time," I say. "It's like a hallway."

"A hallway?"

"Yeah," I say.

"Like at school?" Sarah C asks.

"Okay, but there's no lockers," I say. "It's just a hallway and there's all these doors. But they're closed. So you've got to decide which ones to open and which ones

I'm so shaken up her pessimistic outpouring that my jaw drops open. A light breeze blows into the pocket of my mouth.

She stops the siren sound.

"It's not about the theft," I say. At least that's what Sarah A always says. "It's about the bond. The sisterhood."

"We could get tattoos."

This idea makes me frown. I'm not sure that I want a tattoo. And because Sarah C has the highest GPA out of all the Sarahs and also scored 2300 on the SAT, sometimes her suggestions carry weight.

"Why would we want to put identifying markers on our bodies?" I ask.

"Good point," Sarah C says. "In a lineup we'd be so screwed."

"A lineup?" I ask.

"Yeah, don't you watch cop shows?" Sarah C asks.

"You have time to watch cop shows?" I ask.

I'm surprised to hear this because being a Sarah takes up all my free time.

"This probably isn't the best time to ponder cop shows," Sarah C say. "The criminals usually get locked up."

"Yeah," I say. "Let's ponder something positive."

There's a long silence.

"Can't you think of anything positive?" I ask.

to walk past. But you never know what you're missing or what you're getting until you've already gotten it," I say.

Sarah C doesn't say anything right away.

"That's a very interior metaphor. I spend a lot of time outdoors. That comparison doesn't really work for me," Sarah C says.

"*My life* is like a hallway," I say.

"That's tragic. I really dig trees," Sarah C says.

I turn and look at Sarah C in the backseat. She's twisting a small section of her red hair around her pointer finger.

"Didn't Sarah A tell you to keep your hair pulled back into a ponytail?" I ask.

"She did, but it makes my neck look so long."

"Aren't swan necks considered attractive?" I ask.

"Maybe. But I like my hair down."

"Sarah C, remember the Oreos," I say.

I turn back to face the front and look out the windshield. I'm thirsty. But I never consume any fluid for at least four hours before a hit. Too much anxiety triggers my pee reflex. I can hear the sound of an elastic band snapping itself into place. Sarah A thinks ponytails look wholesome. She thinks it's the right message to send.

"You've got two more minutes," I say.

"I know. I'm going to ask for help in the magazine section. I'm interested in buying a Spanish copy of *People*."

"But you're not going to *buy* it," I say.

"I know. I'm going to act extremely disappointed by the cover and pretend that I wanted the issue containing *los cincuenta mas bellos.*"

"I thought Sarah A said to trill your *R*'s," I say.

"There aren't any *R*'s in the phrase *los cincuenta mas bellos,*" she says.

She makes a valid point.

"Maybe you should follow up by saying *muchas gracias* and trill that *R*."

"I'm not trying to sound like I'm an actual Spaniard. I'm supposedly buying it for a summer school report. Overdone inflection might make a clerk suspicious."

"Don't get mad at me. These are Sarah A's instructions," I say.

She doesn't respond. We sit in uncomfortable silence. Sometimes I think Sarah C misses the bigger picture about being a Sarah. It's as if she mixes up the idea that we're good people who sometimes do bad things with the idea that we're deeply flawed people driven to commit deplorable acts on a daily basis. I might have to talk with Sarah A about this again. Last time I brought up Sarah C's negative attitude with Sarah A, I was left with the impression that Sarah A was growing concerned about our group of four.